I0781100

Necromancer

Coven: Book 11

David Neth

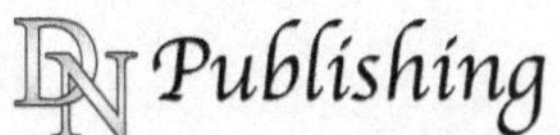
DN Publishing

Necromancer
Coven, Book 11
Copyright © 2024 by David Neth
Batavia, NY

www.DavidNethBooks.com

ISBN: 978-1-963602-14-2
First Edition

Subscribe to the author's newsletter for updates and exclusive content:
DavidNethBooks.com/Newsletter

Follow the author at:
www.facebook.com/DavidNethBooks
www.instagram.com/dnpublishing
patreon.com/DNPublishing

Also by David Neth

<u>Lost By Magic</u>
Lost By Magic
Lucky By Magic
Lured By Magic

<u>Coven</u>
Harpy
Siren
Valkyrie
Shapeshifter
Sorcerer
Witch (Short Story)
Enchantress
Oracle
Trickster
Poltergeist
Hex (Short Story)
Witch Hunter
Demon (Short Story)
Necromancer
Psychic (Short Story)
Incubus

<u>Under the Moon</u>
The Full Moon
The Harvest Moon
The Blood Moon
The Crescent Moon
The Blue Moon

The Art of Magic

<u>Under the Moon: Villains</u>
Toxanna (Short Story)
The Queen (Short Story)
The Dark Knight (Short Story)

<u>Fuse</u>
Origin
Omertá
Oblivion

<u>Heat</u>
Black Magnet
Dust Storm
The Gatekeeper

<u>Standalone</u>
All I Ever Wanted

CHAPTER 1

- BEFORE -

Marie felt a chill hit her skin immediately. She rolled onto her back, groaning with the effort. Her hands traced over her arms, checking to make sure they were still intact. The flames that she had been consumed in only moments before had been torture, but they apparently left no physical scars on her body.

Her eyes cracked open and what she saw made whatever relief she had felt melt into dread.

Standing over her, Credan Graeme smiled.

"Hello, darling." He extended his hand to her. "You're free, yet again."

Marie ignored his hand and pushed herself to her feet. She wobbled slightly, but kept her eyes locked on Credan the whole time. She didn't want to accept his help for anything.

The look of distaste she offered him did nothing to deter him. He stepped toward her and attempted to take her into his arms.

She swatted him away and took a step backward. "What do you want this time?"

The rejection seemed to amuse him. "I love your feisty spirit, dear."

Marie stepped around him and turned her back to him. "Why won't you just leave me alone?"

"Because we're in love," he said plainly. "You just haven't realized it yet."

Her mind immediately filled with thoughts of her husband, Frankie, and the wonderful—albeit short—marriage they had had. "I could never love you."

That seemed to irritate him. He let out a groan—almost a growl—and said in a very controlled tone, "*Sweetheart.* With what you're up against, you're just mourning the life you had."

She whirled around on him. "I can mourn the life I had, *and* be sure that I don't love you."

Credan ground his teeth. "Is this the thanks I get for saving you from eternal damnation? You should be grateful."

"I didn't ask to be plucked out of the billions of other souls trapped in hell."

He shook his head. "I disagree. Your spirit stuck out to me, among all of the other souls. After twenty years, you're still so full of life. That tells me two things: one, that you truly don't belong here."

Marie studied him. He had her hooked. "And the other?"

"That you have great power."

She scoffed. "Of course. Power. That's all you people are after. That's the only reason you're doing any of this. If it's my power you're after, why don't you just obliterate my spirit and take it from me? Why do you need to keep dragging me out of hell, only to shove me back in until you're ready for me again?"

Credan's face softened and he took a step toward her. "Sweetheart, I do it because I love you." He tried to reach for her again, but she swatted his arms away. This time, he only looked disappointed. "Your soul is what drew my attention. Your shine. There's something special about you. That's why, from the moment I pulled you out of the sea of tortured souls, I fell in love with yours."

She shook her head and stepped away from him. "You don't even know what love is."

"Yes, I do," he insisted. "I've never felt this way about a soul before."

"That doesn't mean that it's love," she said. "Are you even capable of love?"

Again, he ground his teeth, making every effort to maintain his composure. "You know, I could return you to your loved ones."

Her head snapped back toward him, her eyebrows raised in attention.

"Would that prove my love for you?"

Marie remained skeptical, eyeing him with nervous anticipation.

Credan began pacing the room, reveling in the fact that he had her hooked. "You have two daughters. They're grown adults now. They've seemed to have done quite well for themselves, from what I can tell. One of them is even a mother herself."

"You better not hurt them," Marie warned.

Credan laughed. "Oh, darling. You're so cute to threaten me. The truth is, there is nothing that you can do that would hurt me. You're just a soul. Without me, you're just another sinner floating in the sea of despair, sentenced to an afterlife of endless torment."

Marie remembered the pain she had endured. The flames licking her skin. The tortured thoughts. The missed moments and memories with her family. Her absence in their lives was enough to send her into a tailspin.

"Unless," Credan went on, "you're willing to help me. What do you say? Are you willing to assist me so that the two of us can be together in life? Or would you rather spend the rest of eternity burning in the flames of hell? The choice is yours, sweetheart."

CHAPTER 2

- APRIL 1990 -

Samantha reached over and wiped the drool from baby Josh's face at the high chair. He wore a light blue bib that said, "Daddy's best friend" on it.

"I'm so happy for you, man," Ryan said from beside his cousin.

Steven beamed at his son, then looked back at Ryan. "Thanks. We're happy you finally made it up here for a visit."

Ryan turned back to his dinner. Chicken Parmesan, which Samantha had spent the last hour cooking. "Yeah, the last year or so has been insanely busy, but I finally got my boat up and running."

"Do you live on the coast?" Samantha asked.

Ryan nodded as he chewed his food. He swallowed, then

said, "Yeah, just outside of Wilmington. A place called Wrightsville Beach. It's pretty quiet this time of year, outside of the few spring break weeks. But in the summers it really blows up. Can't beat the views, though. And it's the best place for my boat."

Ryan lived in North Carolina, where he had moved with his family when he and Steven were fourteen. Before that, the two of them had been inseparable, due to their close age and the fact that they both didn't have any siblings. Their uncanny resemblance to one another left many assuming that the two were brothers. Possibly even twins.

"Erie is a waterfront city," Steven said.

Samantha scoffed. "It's not exactly oceanfront, though."

Ryan nodded. "Erie seems nice, though."

"It is," she conceded. "I love it here, but it's nothing like North Carolina." She looked over at her husband. "Maybe for one of our anniversaries we can go somewhere coastal like Wrightsville Beach."

Steven shrugged and dug into his food. "Yeah, maybe."

Their first anniversary had passed without much fanfare from the two of them, thanks in large part to Josh's arrival the month before. At the time, the doctor hadn't given Samantha the go-ahead to return to the bedroom with her husband, and now that they had missed their anniversary and Valentine's Day, part of their romance had fizzled a bit. They were still trying to figure out how to be parents in addition to husband and wife.

"I hope you don't mind the spare bedroom," Samantha said. "It's pretty sparse, since my sister moved out. She needed to take the bed and the dresser and everything. When you said you were coming, we got a daybed to put in there, so I hope it's comfortable."

"I'm sure it'll be fine," he said. "The room seems very nice."

"Hey, did you—" Steven started, but stopped when they heard a very *distinct* sound emanating from Josh, followed by a smell that made the three adults cover their noses.

Samantha laughed and looked to her son. "Feel better, Josh?"

Steven swatted at the air in front of his nose. "Woo, that's ripe!"

Samantha was already standing, pulling Josh out of the high chair. "Come here, baby. Let's get you cleaned up. You're probably getting ready for your bottle, too."

She carried him into the living room, where they had set up a changing table. There was another one in his bedroom, but this way they didn't have to keep running up and down the stairs whenever Josh needed changing.

As she cleaned up her son, she heard Steven ask Ryan, "Hey, do you want a beer?" A minute later, she heard two cans cracking open, and the furniture creaking as Steven made himself comfortable at the dining room table.

With Josh all clean, she rested him against her shoulder and shushed him as he started whimpering. She patted his back as she bypassed the two men in the dining room and went straight for the kitchen to grab a pre-made bottle from the fridge.

Carrying it back to her seat at the table, she propped Josh in the crook of her arm and fed him the bottle, which he sucked down hungrily. A small stream of formula dribbled from his mouth and down his cheek, which Samantha wiped up with the burp cloth.

"You're a complete natural," Ryan admired from across the table.

Samantha smiled. "Thanks. It doesn't take long to pick this stuff up, even though I still feel like I'm making things up as I go along."

Steven smiled. "She's a fantastic mother."

The compliment both surprised and touched Samantha, who couldn't find a better response other than to return the smile.

"What about you?" Steven asked Ryan. "Got a girlfriend or anything?"

"No, I've been too busy," he said. "Honestly, I've been working overtime, fixing up other people's boats so that I can pay for the repairs on mine. The only way I could even afford a boat in the first place was to get one that needed work. Took me well over a year to get it operational. When I get back, I plan on taking it on a two-week trip down the coast."

"That sounds nice," Samantha said. "Your boss lets you take that much time off? I mean, you're here for a week, and then you'll be gone for another two?"

Samantha, herself, was at the end of her maternity leave. Ryan's visit was almost a little ill-timed, being that she was set to go back to work on Monday. She felt better that Steven had the following week off, so he could take care of Josh and she would only be a phone call away if something happened. Still, the idea of going back to work—and being away from her baby—was one that filled her with dread.

"I'm more freelance," he said. "I've been saving up for a while for this. I'm not really a nine-to-five kind of guy, so this actually works better for me."

Samantha laughed. "You sound like my sister." As she raised Josh back to her shoulder to burp him, she felt him spit up all over. Moments later, she felt the regurgitated milk soak into her shirt.

Steven made a face. "Ugh, the smell!"

Sighing, she rose to her feet again. "I'll take care of it."

"Do you need any help?" Ryan offered.

"No, it's fine." She disappeared through the kitchen and into the back room, where the washer and dryer were. Setting Josh on a towel on the floor, she carefully stripped off his onesie and threw it in the washer. Then she pulled off her shirt and did the same, before reaching for another one.

Just as she was redressing, Kathy came in through the back door with a laundry basket propped on her hip.

"Oh, hi! What are you doing down there?" She leaned over

and made a face at Josh.

Samantha picked him up and propped him on her hip. "He just spit up the bottle I gave him."

"Are you getting sick?" Kathy made a face at her nephew and tickled his belly, which he giggled at.

"No, just spit up. That's what babies do sometimes. Meanwhile, Steven just sat there and gagged. Glad he was helpful."

Kathy set her basket on the dryer. "Isn't his cousin visiting? Steven deserves a break too."

"He hasn't been the one taking care of Josh twenty-four-seven for the last four months."

"That's not exactly fair," Kathy countered. "He helps. But he can't take maternity leave like you. Besides, he has next week off, so he'll get a taste of what you've been dealing with."

"I suppose." Samantha handed Josh to her sister and then applied the soap to the washer before starting it. "I just wish I would get a little help when he got home, you know?"

"Is this still about the sex thing?"

Samantha turned away, regretting telling her sister about the intimate details of her marriage.

"Honey, you guys will figure it out. And you'll figure out the parenting thing too. It'll just take time." Kathy bounced Josh and made faces at him, smiling even more when he giggled. "Do you want me to take him for a day? Maybe you and Steven could—"

Samantha put up her hands to stop her sister. "Ew, no. The

last thing that will put me in the mood is having my sister babysit so my husband and I can have sex."

Kathy shrugged. "You're the one that put it that way. What you two do when I have Josh is on you. I don't need to know the details."

"*Anyway*," Samantha said to change the subject. "It's getting late. I should probably take Josh upstairs and give him a bath, then put him to bed."

Kathy smushed her face to Josh's and kissed his cheek. "Okay, baby! I love you! I love you! I love you! Goodnight!"

Samantha pried Josh away from her sister. "Let's not suffocate the kid, Kathy." Taking hold of Josh's hand, she waved it toward Kathy. "Josh, can you say, 'Goodnight, Aunt Kathy!'"

"That still sounds so weird to me," Kathy said. "*Aunt* Kathy."

"Well, that's what you are now. Just like I'm *Mom*."

Kathy grinned. "Now *that* sounds weird."

"Just pile it on to all of the other changes." Samantha started back into the house.

"Hey, do you want me to say something to Steven? About helping out?"

Samantha shook her head. "No. Not unless it comes up." She paused, then turned back to her sister. "Or maybe just remind him that since I took the evening shift with Josh, he needs to take the overnight shift."

Kathy saluted. "Yes, ma'am!"

The girls made their way to the dining room, which was

now empty. Steven and Ryan's voices carried in from the sunroom.

Kathy walked in and greeted Steven, then extended her hand to Ryan. "Hi, I'm Kathy. Samantha's sister." When she laid her eyes on Ryan, she was immediately taken with him. He looked like Steven, sure, but there was a very clear difference. One that she found endearing.

Ryan smiled at her and shook her hand. "Nice to meet you. Samantha and Steven have said a lot about you."

Kathy blushed and rubbed the back of her neck. "Oh my. Hopefully only good things."

"Let's just say, I'm *very* pleased to meet you."

CHAPTER 3

"More coffee?" Kathy brought the pot over to the kitchen table and refilled Ryan's mug.

"Thank you," Ryan said.

"You're welcome." She smiled down at him.

Steven extended his own mug and, as an afterthought, she refilled his as well.

"You know, don't you have your own apartment?" Steven asked.

"I just stopped over to finish my laundry," she said. "Besides, with my birthday tomorrow, I took the day off. Everyone else is working except for you guys, so I figured I'd spend my pre-birthday with my family."

Samantha was set to return to work on Monday after having

nearly four months off for maternity leave. And Steven had taken time off for Ryan's visit, so it was an unusual Friday morning at home.

"Tomorrow's your birthday?" Ryan asked.

Kathy beamed. "Yup. I'll be twenty-three."

"My birthday was a month ago to the day."

"How old?"

"Twenty-five."

"Hmm," Kathy murmured with a grin. "Not that much of an age difference."

Samantha stepped into the room with Josh on her hip. "Didn't you move out?"

"That's what I told her!" Steven waved his coffee mug at her.

"It's my day off and I have laundry to finish." Kathy took the seat next to Ryan and leaned toward him. "How long are you here for?"

Samantha pulled a bottle out of the fridge. As soon as Josh saw it, he began puckering his lips and whining for it. In the time it took Samantha to cross the room and take her own seat at the table, Josh was nearly wailing, afraid that he wouldn't get to drink his morning bottle.

Steven covered his ears. "Josh! Stop it! I have a headache."

Samantha glared over at her husband. "He can't help it. He's hungry." She put the bottle in her son's mouth and the crying immediately stopped as he sucked down the formula.

Steven leaned on the table, rubbing his forehead. "I haven't drank that much since our wedding."

"Sorry," Kathy said coyly. "I should've left after the first two drinks."

"How late were you here last night?" Samantha asked her sister.

"I think I left about midnight."

"You were here that whole time? Doing *what?*"

Kathy nodded toward Ryan. "Just…getting to know each other."

"All right." Samantha stood and handed Josh over to Steven. "Take him. I need to talk to my sister in the other room. Oh, and don't forget to burp him! Otherwise he's going to spit up all over himself like he did last night."

Steven looked defeated, but he took his son anyway while the girls left the room.

In the dining room, Samantha swatted at her sister's arm. "What are you doing?"

"Ow!" Kathy recoiled. "I was just talking!"

"No, you've been flirting. With my husband's cousin, who could easily pass as his twin." Samantha made a face. "That's just gross!"

Kathy rolled her eyes. "It's not like I suddenly have the hots for Steven, Sam. You can calm down."

"Then what is it? Last I knew you were on a dating-detox. It's only been a couple months since the last guy you dated. What was that one's name? Malcolm?"

"Michael. That ended before it could really start, so that doesn't even count," Kathy said. "If you want to get technical, I haven't been with someone since Jeremy, and those couple months have been lonely. I live alone, Sam. It'd be nice to have someone to talk to."

"You can talk to me."

"And talk about Josh? Or listen to you complain about Steven?"

"I don't complain about Steven…*all* the time."

Kathy nodded. "You kind of do, Sam. I get it, a new baby brings stress to a marriage, but you two are going to have to find a way to work it out. Go to counseling. Have a date night—get laid! Do something!"

"Sorry."

"It's okay. It just…doesn't leave a lot of room for you and me," Kathy said. "I'm so happy for you and your family, but I'm your family too."

Samantha pulled Kathy in for a hug. "I know. And I'm sorry if you've been feeling neglected. I'll try to include you more." As they parted, Samantha added, "But I still don't like this thing going on between you and Ryan. Like I said, he and Steven could be twins. I hope for your sake that looks is all they share."

Kathy raised her eyebrows. "You're doing it again, Sam."

"Sorry. It's just hard for me to *not* vent about him when it seems like I'm the only one doing the work around here. I mean, he never even got up for Josh's one o'clock feeding because he was still down here getting drunk with Ryan!"

"At least he wasn't at the bar and racking up a bill."

Samantha shot her a look. "That's not much better."

"Okay, drinking aside, Steven said he and his cousin used to be really close, right?"

She nodded. "Almost like brothers, yeah."

"And what do you think you and I would be doing if we hadn't seen each other in years? We'd be chatting and catching up into the late hours."

Samantha considered it, then let out a sigh. "I guess you're right. But this has been happening before Ryan came to stay with us."

"So talk to your husband about it," Kathy said. "Share your expectations of each other with *each other* and not with innocent third-parties."

"That's some pretty wise advice for someone who can't keep a boyfriend."

Kathy's jaw dropped in surprise. "Hey, they can't hold on to *me*. Not the other way around."

Samantha laughed.

"Look, you don't have to worry about me and Ryan," Kathy went on. "I'm not trying to form a long-term relationship with him. He's going back to North Carolina next week, so what's the harm in having a little fun while he's here? Give me a break from the loneliness."

"You know, if you're lonely, you can always move back in here."

The younger sister laughed. "Sure. Steven would *really* go for that. Besides, there are some types of lonely that a sisterly chat just can't cure."

Samantha made a face. "Ew."

Kathy laughed again and started back toward the kitchen. "It's just fun. I promise! You should try it sometime!" She disappeared through the door, leaving Samantha alone in the dining room.

The older sister was about to rejoin her family in the kitchen when she heard the doorbell ring. Samantha checked her watch and saw that it was just after eight. Still a little early for house calls, but not unheard of, either. She only hoped it wasn't a door-to-door salesman or a Jehovah's Witness.

She crossed the foyer and opened the large oak door, and had to grip the door to steady herself when she saw who was on the other side. After a moment, she could only choke out one word:

"Mom."

CHAPTER 4

Samantha stood frozen, staring at the face she mostly only remembered from pictures. Even with all of the supernatural experiences that she had witnessed in her life, seeing her mother standing in front of her was one of the most surreal ones that Samantha had a hard time pulling herself from.

Marie stepped forward. "Oh, Samantha! How you've grown!"

Those simple words were enough to break through Samantha's stunned expression. She broke down in tears and collapsed into her mother's arms.

Marie hugged her daughter tight, tears streaming down her own eyes as well. "Oh, baby girl, I've missed you so much!" She pulled away, long enough to cup Samantha's face in her hands, then pulled her in for another hug.

"What's going on?" Samantha asked. "How are you here? How is this possible? Where did you come from?"

"There will be plenty of time for all of that later. It's just so good to see you!"

"Oh, Mom. I've missed you!" Samantha laughed as she wiped away her tears. She turned back toward the house. "Kathy! Come out here!"

Marie held her daughter's face in her hands and studied her. "Oh, my darling, look at the grown woman you've become!"

"What is…it?" Kathy called from the kitchen. But her voice trailed off. Samantha and Marie both turned to look in her direction and saw her frozen there, at the end of the dining room table, keeping her distance.

"Kathy," Samantha choked between tears, "it's Mom!"

Immediately, Kathy darted across the room and into her mother's arms. They held each other close as they all shed tears. Finally, Marie waved Samantha in so the three of them were locked in an embrace.

"I've dreamed of this moment, but I never thought it would come true," Kathy confessed. "This is…you're…"

Marie laughed and pulled away to wipe at her face. "Me too, sweetheart."

Samantha nodded to the living room. "Come on. Let's sit down. We have so much to catch up on."

The three women moved to the couch, all of them attempting to dry their tears that continued to flow. Samantha and Kathy sat on either side of their mother on the couch, none of them daring to be any farther from each other than they needed to be.

Marie held their hands and looked back and forth between the two of them. "Okay. Catch me up on the last twenty years. What have you both been doing? What's life like now in…what year is it?"

"It's 1990," Kathy said.

"Oh my, it certainly has been a while."

Samantha nodded. "I'm a mom now. Little Josh is almost four months old. And I'm married! We just celebrated our one year anniversary in January. Oh, and I graduated college and got a job!" The words rattled off her tongue in quick succession.

"That's wonderful, dear!" Marie beamed. "Oh, I'm so glad to hear it! I knew you'd do great things in life!" She turned to her younger daughter. "And what about you, my sweet baby girl? Married?"

Kathy shook her head. "No, not yet. I'm single."

"And making the most of it, I'm sure!"

"You could say that," Samantha murmured.

Kathy swatted at her, which brought laughter to Marie.

"Oh, I love how the two of you are still such close sisters!"

"Yeah, we're good," Kathy said. "Fighting off evil will bring you closer together."

"I bet they're all afraid of you by now."

"Doesn't stop them from trying to come after us," Samantha said.

Marie squeezed their hands. "I'm just so proud of the two of you. And I'm so happy to see the two of you as adults! I wish I hadn't missed all the years in between."

"About that—" Kathy started.

"So!" Marie cut in. "When do I get to meet this grandchild of mine? Josh, you said his name was?"

Samantha nodded. "Yeah. He's pretty great."

"And your husband? What's his name?"

"Steven."

"And you say you've been married for a year?"

"Almost a year and a half, at this point," Kathy said.

"He takes care of you?" Marie asked her daughter.

Samantha nodded and shrugged. "For the most part, yeah."

Kathy rolled her eyes. "He makes her very happy. They're just going through some post-baby growing pains."

Marie tossed her head back and laughed. "Oh! I know that phase! You two girls came back-to-back, so the post-baby phase lasted a while for me and your father. I've always said, the two of you were born to be sisters and refused to spend very long apart from each other, even right from birth! It's such a blessing to see that you're both still close."

They looked at each other, mother taking in her daughters, daughters studying the mother they had lost.

"So," Kathy said before she could be overcome with emotion

again. "Before we go in to meet Steven and Josh, you should probably know that Steven's cousin Ryan is here visiting, and he's nonmagical."

Marie nodded and mimed locking her lips. "Mum's the word. Got it!"

Samantha stood. "Oh, and he also doesn't know that Josh will one day develop powers of his own, so keep quiet about that too."

"You're lying to your husband about your son's destiny?"

"That's what I said!" Kathy added.

"I'm not lying, I'm just letting him believe what he wants to believe to make him feel better."

Marie eyed her daughter. "I know you know better than that."

Samantha looked between Marie and Kathy. "Sheesh, she's back for ten minutes and she's already mothering."

"That never goes away, dear. You'll learn that soon enough. Now, the suspense is killing me. I would love to meet my grandson!"

Samantha took her mother's hand. "You know, ever since I became pregnant, I never thought you'd meet my children."

Marie smiled. "With magic, anything is possible."

CHAPTER 5

Marie bounced Josh in her lap and made faces to try to get him to laugh. Samantha sat beside them, taking in the multi-generational greeting that she thought would be impossible for so long.

Kathy stood back near the kitchen counter with Steven and Ryan. She would get her time to be alone with her mother. Now was Samantha's time. Besides, Samantha at least had *some* memories of their mother, whereas Kathy had none. This reunion was more monumental for the older sister in that regard.

Ryan leaned over to Steven. "Not to be disrespectful, but I thought that Samantha's mother had passed away?"

Steven's mouth opened in a desperate attempt to come up with an explanation.

Kathy saw him struggle and leaned in closer to Ryan to whisper. "Our mother…*left* when we were little, yes. We haven't seen her in twenty years."

"So she wasn't dead?" Ryan asked.

The witch didn't want to lie, so instead she indicated Marie with her eyes. "Does she look dead to you?"

Ryan seemed confused. "Um…no. I guess not. I must've…been thinking about somebody else."

Kathy could tell that Ryan didn't completely believe her explanation, but there was no use arguing when Marie was standing right in front of them. Kathy, meanwhile, knew that she was on some thin ice, as far as explanations were concerned. For one, if she and Ryan had any sort of future—even a short, fun week together—then lies and deception were not the way to proceed with that. And two, Ryan was Steven's cousin. Technically he was Samantha's family now. What he thought about their mother mattered because it would mean that Samantha would possibly need to keep up the lie later.

"Well," Ryan said with a sigh. "I should go get dressed and leave you guys alone to enjoy some family time."

"Take advantage of that free shower while you can," Steven said. "Sharing one full bathroom with all of these people can get tricky." He grinned at Kathy, remembering that time nearly two years ago when Kathy had accidentally walked in on Steven in the shower. Back before he knew they were witches.

"That's the plan," Ryan said. He looked at Kathy and nodded

toward the door. "Can I talk to you alone for a quick sec?"

"Uh…sure!" Kathy smiled at her mother and sister as she power-walked into the dining room, where Ryan stood waiting for her in his pajamas. "Is this a secret rendezvous?" she asked him when they were alone.

Ryan seemed a bit uncomfortable, which altered Kathy's mood.

She became every serious. "Sorry. I didn't mean to imply that—what's up?"

He looked down at himself and chuckled. "What great timing, you know? I still have bedhead and you've just been reunited with your mother." He shook his head. "You know what? Never mind. Forget I said anything." He turned to head toward the stairs, but Kathy caught his arm and held it.

"Freeze!" The irony of the comment, which matched her power, was not lost on her. "You're not getting away that easy. Spill."

Ryan turned to face her again. "Are you sure this isn't a bad time? I don't want to interfere with your mother being back in town. Not when I'm going back to North Carolina next week."

"Ryan, trust me, it's fine." Kathy grinned to show him that it was. "What is it?"

"Well, I have to be honest. Last night when I was catching up with Steven, I was a little annoyed that you decided to join us."

She dropped his arm and looked away. "Oh."

"*At first*, that is," he added quickly. "And then I started talking to you and getting to know you and…" He rubbed the back of his head and let out a deep breath. "I couldn't stop thinking about you all night."

Kathy met his eyes again. "Yeah?"

He nodded. "And I was so glad to see that you came back this morning."

"Truthfully, *you* were the biggest reason I came back so soon this morning."

That brought a smile to his face. "Well, in that case, would you maybe want to go to dinner with me tonight? Somewhere so we can *really* get to know each other?"

Kathy's first instinct was to shout "Yes!" but she played it cool. She pretended to think about it. "Actually, I think tonight would be perfect. My birthday's tomorrow and if we go tonight, that means that we'll get that awkward first date out of the way so that we can really celebrate with whatever my sister has planned for me tomorrow."

Truthfully, Kathy wondered if her sister had planned *anything*. With Josh still getting up at night, and Samantha returning to work on Monday, Kathy's birthday would likely be an afterthought. And now with their mom returning…

"So…that's a yes?"

She beamed. "Absolutely. I would love to go out with you."

"Good." He leaned in to give her a hug, then stopped

short. "Wait a minute. You said 'first date.' Are you anticipating anymore dates with me?"

Again, she played it coy. "Maybe." Her face broke into a smile. "Let's just say, more dates is a very real possibility."

CHAPTER 6

Cassandra was agitated as she burst through the door onto the street. The day was surprisingly warm, for a spring day. The sunshine only lifted her mood a little, though. She had been stalling, killing time waiting for Talia to finish getting ready so they could open the shop.

Finally, Cassandra had told her that she'd go down and open up and Talia could come down whenever she was ready. It was a good thing they lived just above the occult shop that they owned. They usually didn't like to open the shop alone, being that they were an "alternative" couple in a neighborhood that had soured a little. But with the sun shining—and with her annoyance growing rapidly—Cassandra thought that she could risk it just this once. After all, nothing bad had happened yet.

Necromancer

Their fears were probably just paranoia.

Fishing her keys out of her pocket down on the sidewalk, Cassandra searched for the right one as she rounded the corner to the front of the shop. She checked the time on her watch. Two minutes after ten. The shop was supposed to be open at ten, and Cassandra liked to get there fifteen minutes early to get things set up and cast some protection spells to create the sense of magical harmony in the shop for their customers. Now she'd have to juggle that on top of handling customers, leaving the shop vulnerable if the ritual went unfinished.

Then again, that too was probably just paranoia.

As she came to the front of the shop, she nearly collided with a large man standing outside it.

"Oh, I'm sorry!" she said. "I didn't see you there. I'm kind of in a rush this morning."

The man didn't respond, which prompted Cassandra to take a closer look at him as a sinking feeling arose in the pit of her stomach.

Not only was he tall, but he was stocky too. And very pale. As if he didn't spend very much time out in the sun. But then, being that it was April, a lot of people were pale after the winter. Still, there was something about the distasteful look in his eyes that made her start to feel a growing sense of dread, as if she instinctively knew that he was a dangerous man.

Without another word, Cassandra slowly turned to return to the apartment. She hadn't locked the door at the street, so if she could get there and get inside, she could deadbolt it and run upstairs and warn Talia. Hopefully escaping to her apartment would be enough for the stranger to walk off. But if not, they would be better equipped for an intruder with their magical instruments in the apartment.

As she started to pick up her pace, he called out to her.

"Are you a witch?"

Cassandra stopped in her tracks. There had been rumors around the neighborhood since they'd opened. Suspicions. Even blatant accusations of witchcraft from those who didn't support the couple or the business they ran, but none of the questions had ever had the certainty that this simple one did.

By the time she turned around, the man was standing uncomfortably close to her. Her heart raced as she considered the distance between herself and the door to her apartment. But she wasn't about to back down and let him see how scared her made her.

The man lifted a large hand and placed it on her chest. Against his flesh, she could feel her heart racing.

Now she tried to run, but she couldn't bring herself to move. Her mind was telling her to escape, but her feet stood immobile.

Then, she felt nothing but pain. She tried to raise her arms to clutch at her heart, but her body suddenly lost all of its strength. Breath had escaped her lungs, leaving her gasping for air. But she couldn't draw another breath, and her gasps for the last desperate attempts to save her life were empty.

Necromancer

She crumpled to the ground, her eyes remained opened, although her vision was fading fast. It barely registered at all with her that she had fallen down. Even her mind was slowing.

The last thought she had, before she succumbed to her demise, was of Talia. Unfortunately, she would be the one to find Cassandra dead on the street. And, oh, how she would carry that with her for the rest of her life.

CHAPTER 7

"Oh, this is cute!" Marie beamed as she looked around Kathy's apartment.

"It's not bad." Kathy carried down an extra pillow, and some blankets from her loft bedroom. She set them on the foldout couch that she had prepared for her mother. "It still doesn't quite feel like home, but it definitely feels like mine."

"I think it's perfect," Marie said.

Samantha came down the stairs quietly. "I think I finally got Josh to sleep."

"I really think you should've left him with Steven," Kathy said. "Especially since he never got up with him last night."

The older sister shrugged. "Yeah, but I wanted Mom to get to spend more time with him. Besides, if Steven didn't get enough sleep last night, he'll have a shorter fuse with Josh and I really don't want Ryan to see that side of him. Not when it only comes out when he's tired."

Kathy disagreed, but let it slide. It was her sister's marriage, not her own. She could handle it however she saw fit.

"What do Steven and Ryan have planned for today?" Marie asked.

"I don't know. But Kathy's right. He deserves to spend time with his cousin. He hasn't been up to visit in a long time."

Marie sat back in her chair. "I admire you for marrying a nonmagical man and trying to keep the secrecy of magic from his family. But doesn't it get tiring?"

"Oh yeah," Kathy murmured as she took a seat on the arm of the chair beside her mother. "It sure does."

Samantha sat at one of the barstools at the kitchen island. "It's just the way things are. That's the price of being a witch nowadays."

"Well, what did Steven say when you first told him that you were a witch?" Marie asked.

"He had…an adjustment period," Samantha admitted.

"He kind of freaked off," Kathy clarified.

"But he decided our relationship was worth it. He's still not too crazy about all of the magic, but I think by now he's learned that I can take care of myself."

Kathy nodded. "He's even helped us a few times with magic-related stuff. There was the poltergeist, when Samantha was possessed. And then we found out or neighbor was a witch hunter. That was stressful."

"Yeah, and I didn't know *that* little tidbit until just recently," Samantha added.

"Well, good for him!" Marie indicated the couch. "So, is this my bed for the foreseeable future?"

"Yeah. Sorry I don't have a separate room for you."

"And sorry I had to kick you out of my house," Samantha said. "With Josh, and Ryan visiting, we've quickly run out of bedrooms."

Marie waved it away. "Oh, that's okay. This will be fine! I'm just so proud of the two of you. Look at what you've done with your lives!"

Kathy toyed with the frayed fabric on her jeans. "It's not much."

"Oh, please! Look at you! This is all yours! And you said you have a job, too."

"Kathy isn't so crazy about her job," Samantha said.

The younger sister shot her a look.

"What?" Samantha said innocently. "It's true. And this is Mom! We should be able to tell her anything."

"Right," Marie added. "Kathy, if something in your life isn't making you happy, then you need to have the courage to make a change."

"What if I don't know what *will* make me happy?"

"Then you create your own happiness."

"Easier said than done," the younger witch murmured.

"Trust me," Marie said. "You don't want your life to end with any regrets."

The room went quiet at the mention of her death. Finally, after several long seconds, Samantha broke the silence. "How long are you—how long will you be staying?"

Marie rubbed the back of her neck. "I'm really not sure."

Samantha exchanged looks with her sister and then turned back to their mother. "Well, how is it even possible that you're here? I mean, you were dead, right? And now you're here. Standing in front of us. Full on flesh-and-bone."

Their mother rolled her eyes and pushed herself up from the couch. "Oh, don't worry about that, dear. The point is, I've returned to you." She walked to the window and looked out at the street below. "This is a great view to people-watch."

"Well, as happy as we are about you being here, Mom," Kathy started, "we're just looking for—"

"You know what we used to do when you girls were little?" Marie cut in, suddenly filled with enthusiasm. "Bake! We should bake something again. Just the three of us. That's a nice quiet thing we can do while Josh sleeps."

Again, the sisters exchanged looks, but Marie pressed on.

"Kathy, do you have the ingredients to make chocolate chip cookies?" Marie walked over to the kitchen and began searching the cabinets. "I don't want to make anything too heavy. Tomorrow we'll be having cake for *someone's* birthday."

"You remembered." That brought a genuine smile to Kathy's face and she rose to join her mother in the kitchen.

"Of course. I could never forget that day. It was when our family was finally complete."

Again, Kathy smiled and gave her mother a sideways hug.

"And you'll be…" Marie tapped her chin and looked to the ceiling as she thought.

"Twenty-three."

Marie's eyes grew wide. "Twenty-three. My, how I've missed so much."

"Twenty years," Samantha said.

"Mom," Kathy started. "There had to have been some kind of *supernatural* element to your return."

Marie turned away from them again. She opened the fridge and gasped. "Eggs! We need eggs! Kathy, how do you survive without eggs?"

The younger witch eyed her mother, then said, "Because I've been eating them."

"Well, we'll need to run to the store to get some."

Samantha slid off the barstool. "I can go. Lord knows I could use a trip to the grocery store by myself for a change."

"How about we all go?" Marie suggested.

The older witch pointed upstairs. "Josh is sleeping, and I really don't want to wake him just to get eggs for cookies."

"How about you two go on without me?" Kathy suggested. "If Mom's going to stay here, I should probably give the apartment a once-over, as far as cleaning is concerned. And that way I'll be here if Josh wakes up."

Samantha grabbed her keys from the counter. "Are you sure you don't mind?"

"Not at all," Kathy said. "The bottles are in the fridge, right? In case Josh wakes up."

Her sister nodded. "Yeah. He's been taking them cold, so you don't need to warm them up or anything. But stop halfway through the bottle and burp him, otherwise he'll spit up the whole thing. Oh, and he's been getting a little bit of a rash, so use some of the cream in the bag. You don't need a lot, but—well, you'll see."

Marie smiled. "You're an excellent mother, Samantha. Not that I'm surprised."

"Thanks."

"I've got everything under control," Kathy said. "Don't worry. Besides, the store is only five minutes away. You'll be back before he wakes up."

Marie gave Kathy a hug and then went to the door. "You ready?"

Samantha stepped toward her sister and hugged her as well. She leaned into Kathy's ear and breathed, "I'll try to get some answers out of her." When they parted, Samantha was all smiles and waved as she and Marie exited.

In the silence that followed their departure, Kathy surveyed the apartment for the best place to start cleaning. She knew the bathroom would need a good scrub, but the silence was also creeping on her. Usually when she was alone, she would put on the TV for some background noise.

Switching it on, she immediately hit the MUTE button, although what showed up on the TV caught her attention. News reporters were standing outside a shop that looked familiar to Kathy. One that she had shopped at many times before.

Mystic Treasures.

Kathy's eyes grew wide and she unmuted it so she could hear.

"…police say one person has died outside of the occult shop at 4th and Walnut streets. The victim has been identified as one of the owners of the shop…"

Kathy dropped the remote when a familiar face showed up on the screen.

Cassandra.

CHAPTER 8

The idea of cleaning went out the window. Kathy wasn't sure how long she sat on the couch watching the newscast, but as she did, she couldn't help but remember how much Cassandra and Talia had helped her and Samantha over the years. Talia had even officiated Samantha's wedding. Not to mention the fact that Cassandra and Kathy were the only two who remembered the alternate timeline that Kathy had created just before Samantha's wedding, when she had accidentally exposed their magic. Thanks to Cassandra, that had been corrected. Now Kathy was the only one who knew.

She watched until one of the afternoon soap operas came on, and then she switched the TV off. Sitting on the couch in the silence, she wiped at her eyes and imagined the commotion of activity on the street that had once been quiet enough to commit a murder.

And Talia. The poor woman must be beside herself. Helpless. Desperate for answers. Scared of being the next victim. Or would she be determined to stop her lover's killer? She was strong, but in moments like these, even the strongest people needed support.

Kathy would be that support.

Springing to her feet, she grabbed her keys and headed toward the door. She needed to be there for Talia. She needed to help figure out what had happened. Her mother and sister would have to understand her sudden absence. She'd explain where she'd gone later.

It wasn't until she had her hand on the doorknob that she remembered Josh, still asleep upstairs. She couldn't leave him.

Pushing down the nagging feeling in her stomach that she was neglecting her duties as a witch, Kathy returned to the kitchen and dropped her keys in the bowl near the stove, where she kept them. If she had to choose between being a witch right now or being an aunt, she had to be an aunt.

Kathy busied herself around the apartment, tidying up, doing everything in her power to try to push aside the thoughts of Cassandra and Talia, but it was impossible.

Ten minutes later, Samantha and Marie returned with a small bag filled with groceries.

"We're back!" Marie trilled as she walked in.

Kathy offered a sad smile.

"What's wrong?" Samantha asked.

The younger sister quickly glanced at her mother, who was emptying the contents of the shopping bag into the fridge. Quietly, she murmured, "I'll tell you later."

"Oh, Kathy," Marie said when she was done in the fridge. "Your sister and I have decided to throw you a birthday party tomorrow night."

"Mom, you don't have to—"

"Nonsense. I'm your mother and I love you. Besides, I've missed the last twenty birthdays, let's celebrate this one!"

Kathy looked over at her sister. "You're okay with this?"

"It'll be at the house, so I can put Josh to bed whenever. Probably just us—"

"Oh, and that gentleman friend of yours from this morning!" Marie added. "Make sure he comes."

"Ryan?" Kathy asked.

"Yes! He's cute."

"Mom!" Samantha blurted. "He looks just like Steven!"

"So you agree. He's very handsome."

Samantha rolled her eyes. "I'm only letting Ryan come because he's staying with us and it'd be rude *not* to invite him."

"Sam, dear, it's your sister's birthday," Marie scolded. "Let her live a little!"

Kathy couldn't help but smile at that.

"How has Josh been?" Samantha asked, just to change the subject.

"Quiet as a mouse." No sooner had the words left her mouth than Josh began to cry from the bedroom upstairs.

"You were saying?" Samantha asked with a chuckle. "It's probably all the sudden chatter. I can get him back down."

"No!" Kathy blurted.

Both women looked at her with surprise.

"Maybe Mom should go," Kathy suggested. "I'm just saying, she deserves to spend more time with her grandson."

"Oh, I would love to," Marie said. Before Samantha could object, she already started toward the stairs.

With their mother gone, Samantha turned to her sister. Kathy grabbed her by the wrist and pulled her into the bathroom, promptly shutting the door behind them. It was the only private place in the whole apartment.

"What's going on?" Samantha demanded.

"Cassandra's dead," Kathy blurted. "Murdered, I presume. By something demonic."

Samantha closed her eyes. "Wait a minute, slow down. Cassandra? From Mystic Treasures?"

Kathy nodded. "Yeah. I saw it on the news after you guys left. Someone found her this morning. From what they're saying, the attack happened late this morning, around ten."

"That's…really sad. We should send Talia flowers."

"No, that's not good enough. We need to find her killer."

"Did the police say that she was murdered?"

"They didn't have to, Sam. She was perfectly healthy and then she just dropped dead on the street."

"That's happened before. There has to be some logical explanation for this."

"Yes. And that explanation you're looking for is that it's a demon who killed her."

Samantha tucked her hair behind her ears and crossed her arms. "Kathy, I need you to listen to me. This is none of our business."

"A demon isn't our business?"

"We don't know that this is a demon!"

Kathy looked away.

Samantha softened her tone. "We've been evil-free for months. I'd like to see that streak continue."

Again, Kathy remained silent. She couldn't help but resent her sister a little bit. The only reason Samantha thought that they'd been evil-free for months was because Kathy had been handling the minor threats to give Samantha time alone with her baby. But Samantha's maternity leave at work was ending, so it needed to end with her witch responsibilities too.

"Turning a blind eye to it does not mean it's not happening," Kathy said. "I mean, Mom's sudden reappearance might even mean that something supernatural is going on that we just haven't figured out yet."

Samantha shook her head. "No, Kathy. Don't do that. Don't

ruin our reunion with Mom, just because you want to go play hero. Cassandra's dead and that's sad. But you don't need to get involved. Leave Talia alone and let her mourn in peace."

CHAPTER 9

"This little boy just wants to see his mommy," Marie said as she carried Josh back downstairs.

Samantha smiled at her son and took him in her arms. "You didn't sleep very long, mister. Are you going to nap again later for me?"

"How about those cookies?" Marie asked. "Where's your sister?"

"She's—"

"Right here." Kathy came out of the bathroom, but refused to look at her sister.

Fine then, Samantha thought to herself. *Be mad.*

"Mom, I don't know if I'm up for cookies," Kathy started to protest.

"Oh, it'll be fun!" Marie said. "Josh would love to watch us, and it'll give the guys some more time to themselves before we take over the house again."

Samantha couldn't argue with that. "True."

"Okay, Kathy, why don't you get me a large mixing bowl," Marie directed. "Sam, you find the cookie sheets. I'll get the batter going."

As the three of them worked, Samantha kept a careful eye on her mother. She didn't want to be skeptical of her presence, but Kathy's comments only amplified the nagging feeling in Samantha's gut that something wasn't quite right about Marie's sudden reappearance to the world. Now that the shock and excitement over her return had subsided a little, what remained were questions. Ones that Samantha wasn't ready to answer—or even pose—yet.

"So, Mom, what's the last thing you remember before you showed up at our front door this morning?" Samantha tried to ask casually as she rolled some of the batter in her hands and placed it on the cookie sheet.

"I don't know," Marie said. "Why do you ask?" She turned and made a face at Josh, who smiled back in response.

"It's just that, you never really answered us about how you returned, or where you've been." Samantha caught Kathy's eye and the two exchanged looks, communicating an apology without speaking a word.

"Don't worry about that, dear," Marie said. "It's in the past.

What matters is that I'm back now."

"But still, have you—"

The oven timer dinged, and Marie rushed over to it to pull out the latest batch. "Oh, aren't these perfect?"

Samantha tried a different approach for answers. It was one she didn't like using on the people she knew, but sometimes it became necessary.

Telepathically, she tried to probe into her mother's mind. Only, whenever she tried, she faced a magical barrier that prevented her from reading the thoughts of her mother.

What are you hiding, Mom? she wondered.

"Kathy, why don't you put on some music while we work?" Marie suggested. "It's awfully quiet in here."

Samantha was sure it was another excuse for a distraction, but she watched as Kathy crossed the room to her small stereo system and played the radio. Janet Jackson's "Escapade" began playing.

"Oh, this is cool!" Marie smiled as she began dancing as awkwardly as she could. "It's *funky*!"

Josh started giggling, followed by Samantha and Kathy.

"You look ridiculous, Mom," Kathy said.

"But it feels so good to move to the music!" Marie cheered. "Don't take yourselves so serious all the time, girls. Learn to let go and have some fun!"

Kathy began to join in, which brought even more laughter from Josh.

"Come on, Sam!" Kathy said. "Josh loves it!"

Samantha finished rolling the last of the cookie batter on the cookie sheets. "No, I'll just sit here and watch the two of you act like idiots."

Over the sound of the music, Kathy heard the phone ring. She rushed over to the radio to turn it down, then picked up the phone from the receiver in the kitchen.

"Hello?"

Samantha turned to Josh and stuck her tongue out at him and blew raspberries in his direction. He only eyed her suspiciously.

"Fine then," Samantha murmured with a chuckle. "Don't laugh at Mommy."

"I'm sorry, but I don't know if tonight is such a good idea…" Kathy said into the phone.

"Is that Ryan?" Marie asked.

Kathy covered the receiver and nodded.

"Don't you dare be canceling any dates with that man," Marie instructed. "He's a nice boy. Give him a chance. Live a little!"

The idea of Kathy on a date with Ryan didn't sit right with Samantha, but she remained quiet. She had made it known how she felt. Nagging her sister about it was not going to change anything.

"If Kathy's busy with her gentleman friend, I can just have dinner with my other daughter," Marie said. "What do you say,

Sam? Family night at your house?"

As much as Samantha didn't want to see Kathy go on a date with Ryan, having Marie alone for a whole evening where they could freely discuss all things magic was appealing. Maybe she could actually get some answers out of Marie, once and for all.

"Sounds good to me," she said.

"Then it's settled." Marie turned back to Kathy. "You tell that boy that you'll go out with him."

Kathy removed her hand from the phone and lifted it to her mouth again. "Ryan? Sorry about that. I guess I am free to go out tonight."

CHAPTER 10

It was just like the family dinners that Samantha had remembered growing up. Warm and cozy after a full meal, telling stories that made them laugh, and being surrounded by the people that she loved.

The weight of her eyelids and the mess left in the kitchen to clean up barely registered in her mind. She sat back and watched as one of her greatest dreams came true.

Marie cradled Josh in her arms and held the bottle for him, cooing and smiling down at him as he drank and looked up at her with wide eyes. When she looked up at Samantha and Steven, she said, "You'll be happy when you're done with these bottles. Samantha decided when she was ready. As soon as she could hold her head up, it seemed like she was trying to reach for what was on our plates." She laughed. "The day we switched her to real food was the happiest day of her life."

Steven smiled. "I'll just be happy when he can start to feed himself."

"Can you imagine all of that baby food all over the walls?" Samantha cringed at the thought of the mess that was about to hit their household in less than a year. That was one piece of parenting that she wished she could eliminate.

"If he's anything like his mother, he won't want anything to do with those little jars of baby food," Marie said. "You wanted the real stuff, even before you were big enough to have it. Always ambitious."

Samantha looked down at the table. "You make me sound like a cow, Mom."

Marie shook her head. "No. You always knew when you had had enough. Your sister, on the other hand, was the angriest little baby if she didn't get her food right away. Now look at her! The woman is as thin as a rail!"

"She runs every day, and she watches what she eats," Samantha murmured.

"And what's your secret?" Marie asked. "You certainly don't look like a woman who just had a baby four months ago!"

Absently, Samantha reached for her stomach, which was squishier than she would've liked, even though she knew it was from Josh more than anything else. "I'm still in my twenties. That's my secret."

"Give yourself some credit," Steven said. "You look great."

She smirked at her husband, but let the comment go. She would thank him for it later. Maybe. If they could actually figure out how to get back in sync in the bedroom.

When Marie lifted Josh to her shoulder to burp him, he wiggled and whined, even after he let out a loud belch. After a few more seconds, there was a distinct sound that came out of his other end that signaled all of the adults to laugh.

"Here, I'll change him." Samantha shot up to her feet.

Steven held out his hand toward his wife, holding her off. "No, I'll get it. You enjoy the time with your mom."

Marie passed him the baby, and he took Josh into the next room to change his diaper.

"You two are going to be great parents." Marie chuckled. "What am I saying? You already are!" She wiped a tear from the corner of her eye as she looked across the table at her daughter. "I'm just so *proud* of you, Samantha. Look at everything you've accomplished, despite—"

"Where have you been, Mom?" The question took even Samantha by surprise. She didn't expect it to come out so direct, so accusatory. But the doubt that Kathy had put in her mind earlier had been lingering all evening.

Marie furrowed her brow. "I don't know what you mean."

"We've assumed you were dead. That's what Dad told us all those years ago."

"Oh." Marie looked down and picked a fuzz off her pant

leg. "That's what you mean."

"Of course that's what I mean." Samantha let out a deep breath. "Kathy and I spent our whole lives missing you. Celebrating birthdays and holidays and life changes without our mother. Then when Dad left, we were on our own! And now you're suddenly back, pretending like it's perfectly normal that you've been raised from the dead and you seem to expect us to go on like you weren't absent for most of our lives."

Marie's eyes shot to her daughter. She held them for a while before finally asking, "So what are you saying?"

"I want to know the truth, Mom. Were you dead, like we thought? Or was that just a story Dad told us to make us feel better? I mean, *did* you abandon us, just like Dad did eventually? Maybe the two of you ditched the two of us so you could live your lives without us." The more she spoke, the more her voice failed her. By the time she tapered off her speech, the tears had begun to flow.

"Oh honey." Marie stood and came around the table. She took the seat beside her daughter and pulled her into her arms. "No. I would never abandon you girls. I love you with all of my soul. You two are the best things to ever happen to me. And I'm sorry I missed so much of your life, but to see where you girls are in your lives right now fills me with so much pride. If I could only succeed at one thing, I'm glad that it's being your mom."

Samantha knew that her mother had deflected the questions yet again, but she didn't care at the moment. She knew that the harder she pushed, her mother would continue to lie to them. Marie loved them, sure, but apparently not enough to tell them the truth.

For the first time in a long time, Samantha wished that her father would return. If, for no other reason, than the fact that he always told them the truth.

CHAPTER 11

Kathy was distracted at dinner while Ryan asked her the usual first-date questions.

"What do you do for a living?"

"I'm, uh, a secretary. At a doctor's office. A dentist, actually."

"That sounds nice. Did you have to get a degree for that?"

"No."

"Did you go to college?"

"For a bit."

Ryan reached for his glass of water and took a sip. "So, what's your dating history? What am I working with here? Fresh out of a long relationship? Dateless and desperate?" He chuckled to try to lighten the mood, but stopped when Kathy didn't return the sentiment.

Kathy felt a jarring change in questioning, from pleasant to interrogation. "No, I've been single for almost a year. I've had a few dates here and there, but nothing major."

"And before that?"

"My ex and I were together for three years before we broke up for a few months. We got back together for a little while, but it didn't work out." Surprisingly, the mention of Jeremy didn't immediately send her mind into a tailspin. Maybe she was finally getting over him. Or maybe she had too much else on her mind.

"You don't seem like yourself." Ryan leaned his chin on his fists and studied her. "This morning you were very flirty with me. You seemed excited for tonight. And then when I called to reschedule because of your mom, you seemed to be hesitant. Now you just seem…I don't know…distant."

Kathy let out a sigh as she fussed with the cloth napkin on her lap. "I'm sorry."

"What's bothering you? Is it something I did? Something on your mind? What's changed since this morning?"

She fingered the stem of her wine glass. She'd only taken a few sips, but that was enough for her. The last thing she needed was alcohol when she had so much on her mind.

"Is it your mother?"

Funny how a total stranger could pick up on what was truly bothering her. But she couldn't exactly tell him that she feared her mother's sudden reappearance in their lives was the result of some suspicious paranormal activity. So instead, she leaned in to another thing that was bothering her.

"It's just something I saw on the news earlier." She fidgeted with her bracelet as she considered how to broach the subject. "My friend Cassandra was murdered."

Ryan's face dropped. "Oh my God. I'm so sorry. No wonder you were hesitant on the phone. And here I am pushing this date like an *idiot*!"

She reached for his hand across the table and squeezed. "It's okay. You didn't know. The truth is, we were more like acquaintances. But it's still upsetting to hear of someone you know being murdered. That stuff doesn't happen in real life. Only in TV shows and movies."

"Unfortunately, it *does* happen in real life."

Kathy, of course, knew all too well that that was true.

"Of course you're feeling sad about it," he went on. "Do the police know who did it?"

"Not that I've heard. The thing is, I can't help but think about Cassandra's partner, Talia." She met Ryan's eyes and said, "Talia's the one who officiated Samantha and Steven's wedding."

Ryan nodded. "Ah, I see."

"Anyway, Cassandra and Talia weren't married, so I'm sure Talia is having a hell of a time being the grieving partner—and she has every right to be."

"Oh, you're saying they're..." He smirked. "Wow. Steven

said you and your sister weren't traditional, but you're *really* not traditional."

Kathy couldn't help but smile. Sometimes it was nice to embrace the role of the strange girl, and she wore it with a badge of honor. "Cassandra and Talia are good people, no matter what happens in the privacy of their own home."

"Of course. I wasn't implying that they weren't. It's just— you don't really hear much about *those* types of relationships."

Another grin came to her face at his reaction. "I just don't understand why someone would want to hurt her, just because she was trying to live her life."

"Do you know that was the reason she was killed? Because she was a…"

"Lesbian?" Kathy shook her head. "No, but I know they've been ridiculed. And they own an occult shop, so it's not as if the neighbors are welcoming them with open arms as it is."

"Sounds like there's a lot of questions you still have," he said. "And I don't think this is going to go away until you get a little bit of closure."

She scoffed. "Like that's going to happen."

"Hey." He waited until she met his eyes. "Do you want to go see Talia?"

"No," Kathy said reflexively. Then she thought about it for a moment. "Well…maybe. Samantha thinks that I should drop it and let Talia be."

"And what do *you* think?"

She let another sigh escape her. "Honestly? I think I need to talk to Talia." She shook her head. "But she probably has too much going on right now. Samantha's right. I would just be getting in the way."

"Or maybe everyone is thinking the same thing," Ryan countered, "that Talia doesn't need to be bombarded so nobody is going to see her."

"Maybe."

"You said it yourself, these women were facing a lot before this happened. But they had each other to lean on. Now they don't. My guess is that they don't have a lot of people in their corner. Maybe all Talia wants right now is some company."

Kathy thought about that. Ryan was right. From what she knew about Cassandra and Talia, they kept to themselves. They had friendly customers, but none of them were true *friends*, from what Kathy knew. And the thought of Talia sitting alone in that apartment, only one floor up from where the love of her life had been killed, made Kathy's stomach turn.

"Okay. I think we should go see her."

"Then that settles it." Ryan set his napkin on the table and stood. He extended his hand out toward Kathy. "We're going to go see your friend."

CHAPTER 12

"**K**athy wasn't home yet." Samantha closed the door into her bedroom, where her husband was sitting up in bed with the newspaper spread out in front of him.

"That would explain why Ryan isn't back yet. Maybe they went parking somewhere." He grinned at the jab.

She rolled her eyes. "Yes, I suppose it would explain why he's not home yet.."

"I'm surprised you left your mom alone at Kathy's."

Samantha sat on the edge of the bed and pulled off her socks. "I didn't want to, but she insisted she would be fine. And it's almost eleven. Kathy has to be home soon."

Steven reached across the bed and rubbed her back absently. "I think you're forgetting who you're talking about."

She rose and pulled her pajamas out of the dresser. As she undressed, she asked, "Did Josh fuss at all?"

"Nope. Apparently your mom tuckered him out."

"Yeah, and then he'll be up again when *I'm* about to fall asleep."

"He has that sixth sense about him," Steven joked. "Tonight was nice. I liked being able to talk to the woman who I've only heard stories about and seen pictures."

Samantha pulled on her pajamas, and then tossed her dirty clothes in the hamper tucked inside the closet. "Yeah."

"That didn't sound sincere."

She took a seat on the edge of the bed again and shrugged. She reached for her lotion and began applying it to her arms.

"What's wrong? I thought you'd be happy to have her back."

"I am. It's just…I've got so many questions too."

"So ask her."

"I've been trying all day! Kathy too. Mom just has a way of avoiding them all."

Steven moved across the bed and began to rub her shoulders.

"I want to know what kind of magic brought her back. Is it only temporary? Do I need to prepare myself to lose her again? And if she wasn't truly dead, then where the hell has she been?" *Why can't either of our parents stick around?* she wondered, but kept that question to herself.

He hugged her from behind and leaned his head close to

hers. "I'll admit that I even find it a little strange that she's back. But then, I find most of the things you and Kathy do strange."

Samantha let out a tired chuckle. She reached up and held his arms, which were wrapped tightly around her.

"So what's really bothering you about this?" Steven asked. "It's not just the unanswered questions."

"I just have a bad feeling in the pit of my stomach that something bad if lurking beneath the surface here. Something we can't see yet. It's happened before."

He resumed rubbing her shoulders. "And you and Kathy have always figured it out before too."

"But I've never been a *mother* before."

"Ah. So that's the problem."

"Of course it is!" Samantha whirled around to face him. "If my gut is right, this is the first demonic threat I'll have to deal with since Josh was born." She shook her head. "And I'm a little annoyed at Kathy for putting this doubt in my head to begin with."

"You would've picked up on it yourself anyway," he said. "You just said it yourself that you have this feeling in your gut that something isn't right."

"Yeah, I do."

"I don't know how this is going to go over with you, but hear me out: maybe—at least until some of these questions you have start getting answered—maybe your mom should keep her distance from Josh. Just in case."

Samantha closed her eyes and tried to push down the emotion she felt rising up. The feeling that she'd be a horrible daughter for keeping her son away from her mother.

But Steven had a point. For the safety of their child, they needed to be careful. And at the moment, the mystery—and therefore the risk of danger—centered on Samantha's mother.

Still, she couldn't shake the memory that would be stored in her mind forever. The one where her mother so happily held Josh and made him laugh. The one of her loving him, just as she had loved Samantha and Kathy. Samantha didn't want to ruin that, or the memory of it.

She pulled away from her husband so she could pull back the blankets. "I don't know."

"It's just to keep him safe. Just until we figure this out." He folded up the newspaper and tossed it on the floor beside the bed.

"I know. I just hate it." She paused, then added, "I'm not saying no. I'm just saying I'll think about it."

"We need to do more than think about it," Steven said. "If it's one thing I've learned since you told me you were a witch, it's that things can change in an instant around here."

Samantha lay her head on the pillow, facing away from her husband. "I'll talk to Kathy in the morning. Maybe between the two of us we can force our mother to answer these questions. One way or another."

CHAPTER 13

Kathy wondered if she should be doing this. It was late and the street was dark. It was almost hard to believe that all day the place had been swarming with police officers, coroners, and forensics.

A chilly mist began to fall, which helped prompt Kathy to raise her hand and knock on the door loudly three times.

"Talia!" she called. "It's me, Kathy! Kathy Walker!" She glanced over at Ryan and gave him a reassuring smile.

"Give it a few minutes," he encouraged. "She might be sleeping."

No sooner had he said that when they heard footsteps at the top of the stairs inside the apartment. Moments later, the door opened and Talia stood on the other side.

To put it mildly, she looked terrible. He eyes were red and puffy. Her hair had been clipped back out of her face, but was coming loose and several strands hung down around her cheeks. And she was wearing a sweatshirt that Kathy had remembered seeing on Cassandra once when Kathy stopped in to Mystic Treasures.

Kathy stepped forward and wrapped her arms around Talia. "Oh, I'm so sorry to hear about what happened."

Talia hugged her back. "Thank you." She pulled away and wiped at her nose.

"I've been thinking about you all day. I just wanted to stop out and see how you were doing."

"Terribly." Talia crossed her arms and leaned against the doorframe. Then she thought better of it. "Oh, it's raining. Would you like to come in?"

Kathy glanced up at Ryan, then back to Talia. "I wouldn't want to impose."

"Please. I've been ignored all day. I'm so glad you came. I could really use the company."

Nodding, Kathy stepped inside and climbed the stairs up to the apartment with Ryan in tow. Behind them, Talia locked the door and then followed them up.

The apartment was bigger than Kathy had expected. She'd never been inside, but what she saw was a spacious living room with a kitchen in the back. Adjacent to that was the bathroom and a single bedroom. All of it was nicely furnished, from the furniture down to the woodwork.

"This is a beautiful apartment," Kathy commented.

Talia looked around, as if seeing it for the first time. "Oh. Yeah. Cassandra and I loved this place. The location could use some work. Especially now." She took a seat on the couch and curled her legs up under her as she pulled a throw blanket overtop of her lower half.

Kathy took a seat in a nearby chair and Ryan followed suit. "This is Ryan. He's a friend of mine. Actually, he's Steven's cousin. Samantha's husband, you know?"

She nodded once. "I remember. How are they doing?"

"Good. They just had a baby at the end of December."

"That's good to hear." There was no enthusiasm in Talia's voice. It was as if all of her emotion had been drained from her.

Kathy wondered what she was doing. She was here to talk about Cassandra and console Talia and yet she somehow steered the conversation to her nephew.

"How…how's it been?" she asked hesitantly. "Have the police come up with anything?"

Talia frowned and shrugged. "I don't know. Nobody is telling me anything. Everyone—the doctors and nurses at the hospital, and the police—all of them keep referring to me as 'Cassandra's roommate,' or 'a friend.' They say that since I'm not family, they can't give me any details." She broke into sobs and covered her mouth as she cried.

Kathy found a box of tissues and leaned over to hand them

to her. "I'm so sorry. That's terrible of them to keep it all from you."

"There's been no protection offered to me. For all I know, the killer is looking at me next. But since they know who I really was to Cassandra, they're all keeping their distance. I wouldn't be surprised if they secretly hoped that the killer got me next."

"Well. Let's just make sure that doesn't happen." Kathy cleared her throat. "As I said, Ryan is Steven's cousin and he's my…friend. But we, uh, we haven't revealed all of our *secrets* to each other yet."

Both Talia and Ryan looked at her strangely, but then Talia nodded.

"I see."

If Kathy was about to ask Talia questions about Cassandra, she wanted her to tread carefully around Ryan, who had no knowledge of the supernatural.

"What *do* you know about what happened?" Ryan asked. "Maybe we can help you try to make sense of it all."

"Yeah," Kathy encouraged. "Tell us what happened. Start from the beginning."

Talia sighed. "Well, we were getting ready to open the shop. I was late, as usual, and Cassandra was getting snippy with me. I was actually quite annoyed with her too. I snapped. Said she's always rushing me and that she should let me be." She took a deep breath, suppressing another sob. "The last thing I said to her—"

"Doesn't matter," Kathy cut in. "She knows how you felt about her, no matter what happened this morning."

Talia offered her a smile. "Thanks. I wish that helped me feel better, but I can't stop replaying those last moments in my mind."

"So you had an argument this morning?" Ryan asked, trying to get the conversation back on track.

"Yeah. She decided to go down and open the store on her own and I told her I would join her when I was ready." She wiped at her nose with the tissue. "Someone outside must've run up to her and killed her quick."

"Do you know how she died?" Kathy asked.

Talia shook her head. "No. Nobody's told me anything. Not even after I explained that Cassandra has had no contact with her family in years. Not since they found out about me."

Kathy moved over to the couch beside Talia and reached for her hand. "I'm so sorry that you're dealing with this."

"Thanks." She offered the witch a sad smile. "Anyway, from what I saw when I found her, there wasn't any blood. No puncture wounds of any kind, of course I wasn't *looking* for those when I found her. I was too busy thinking about…" She sucked in a shuddering breath, unable to speak the end of the sentence.

"So how do you know someone killed her?" Ryan asked. "Maybe it was just a heart attack or something."

"I overheard a neighbor talking to the police. He said he saw someone walk up to her and reach his hand to her."

"He hit her?" Ryan asked.

Talia shook her head. "That's not what it sounded like."

"So maybe he had nothing to do with—" Ryan started, but Kathy held her hand out to him to signal him to stop.

Her wheels were spinning with possibilities. Her hunch had been right. This was supernatural. Somehow. But Ryan wouldn't understand that, and having the conversation tiptoe around his ignorance to magic would only make Talia frustrated and Kathy wanted to prevent that.

"Do you want to come back and stay with me tonight?" Kathy offered. "My mother is in town, and judging by the time, I think that she's already settled on the couch. But I'd be happy to either share my bed with you or make up a bed on the floor."

For a moment, Kathy considered suggesting Samantha's house. But with Josh still waking up in the night, Kathy didn't want to bring anymore stress—or potential danger—to her sister. Besides, Samantha's bedrooms were all booked up as well.

"That's sweet of you." Talia squeezed her hand back. "But I'd rather stay here with Cassandra's things. It helps me feel closer to her with her gone."

Kathy nodded. "Just make sure you're as *protected* as you can be."

"I've already taken care of it," she said. "That's why I answered the door when you knocked. I could tell it was safe. I wouldn't have done it for anyone else."

Ryan looked at Kathy, confused. She sidestepped his puzzlement by rising to her feet, which Ryan followed.

"Let me know if you need anything," Kathy offered.

"I will. Thank you for coming."

"It was nice meeting you," Ryan said. "Sorry it had to be over such sad circumstances."

Back on the street, Kathy was quiet as she and Ryan walked to the car amid the April drizzle. She felt better after seeing Talia. More determined that Cassandra's death was supernatural. That she could get justice for her that wouldn't come from the police department.

"Do you feel better, now that we came and talked to her?" Ryan asked once they were in the car.

"Very much so." Kathy was going to find out who Cassandra's killer was.

CHAPTER 14

"I'm sorry for ruining our date," Kathy said in the car on the way back to her apartment.

"Nonsense," Ryan said from behind the wheel of his rental. "I had a good time—despite being in the presence of a grieving woman."

"I bet it's the strangest first date you've ever had."

He chuckled. "True. But you going to see Talia after what she's been through showed me more about you and your character than a whole night full of conversation would have. You're a good person, Kathy. You care about people and you're not afraid to show that."

She reached across the center console for his hand. He brought it up to his lips and kissed it.

"Honestly, though, it's awful what happened to Cassandra," Ryan said. "And how everybody is treating Talia."

"I know. I can't believe people can be like that. So stuck in their ways that they can't set aside their differences to comfort a poor woman. To provide her with just the tiniest bit of closure. But no, instead they ride high on their power trip and withhold information just because they can. It's like they're trying to punish Talia for who she loved, *completely* ignoring the fact that she found that person she loved so much *dead* on the street. Hasn't she been through enough? Why add more ridicule?"

Kathy could feel herself getting more worked up as she talked. Not only was it the illogical behavior of magical evil that bothered her, but it was also the blatant disregard for Talia's feelings in all of this.

"I know. I agree. But if the rules say that they can only tell family, then we need to respect that. No matter how dumb it is."

"Screw the rules," Kathy blurted. "This is an abuse of power. This has nothing to do with the rules, or why they were truly created, which is to protect the privacy of the patient. Cassandra has no one else. Talia is the person they should be telling everything to. But they won't, because of who she decided to spend her life with."

"Kathy," Ryan warned, "please don't do anything that you'll regret later. I know you want to help your friend, but these are government entities you're facing. You're not going to change their ways overnight. And think of what you'd be putting Talia through by fighting for it. There's no way to go back in time and change what happened."

Kathy, of course, knew that wasn't true. But the one and only time she had time traveled, it had been with the help of Cassandra. Without her, would it even be possible?

Ryan pulled over on the street in front of Kathy's apartment building. He shifted the car into park and then leaned over toward Kathy.

"Do you want me to walk you to the door?"

Kathy looked out the window and saw that the rain was coming down harder now. "No, that's okay. It's wet outside and I don't want to wake my mother—or risk being interrogated."

He smiled. "I had a good time tonight. Maybe our next one could be a *little* more traditional, though?"

She leaned in and kissed him. "You said it yourself that I'm not a traditional girl."

"That you aren't. When can we do this again?"

"Well, apparently my mother and sister are throwing me a birthday party tomorrow at Samantha's house. You should come."

"Considering that that's where I'm staying, I think I could drop in for a bit."

"As long as you can pencil me in." She grinned and then leaned in and kissed him again. "Goodnight, Ryan. I'll see you tomorrow." She let her hand linger in his as she used her other one to open the car door and step out into the rain.

As she scurried to the door and unlocked it, she realized that she was still smiling. Once inside, she peered through the glass and saw him waving from the car. She waved back and wished that his visit was a much longer stay. Possibly even forever.

CHAPTER 15

Kathy unlocked the door to her apartment and stepped inside. What she walked into was not what she had expected to see.

Marie stood in the kitchen, facing a man that Kathy didn't recognize. He was tall, broad-shouldered, and had the palest skin that Kathy had ever seen. He wore a black pea coat over a white linen shirt.

"Oh," Kathy said when she saw them. "I'm sorry. I didn't realize you were—uh, well, that you were having company." She averted her eyes and started to round the opposite side of the kitchen island to escape from the awkward encounter.

Never in her life did she expect to walk in on her mother with a man.

"You don't have to go, honey," Marie said. "Credan was just leaving."

His name made Kathy stop and meet his eyes. There was something dark about them. Sinister. She didn't like it. And his name was unusual. Not that that meant anything necessarily, but it was noteworthy.

Credan watched as she studied him.

"All right," Marie said to him. "It's time that you get going. This is Kathy's apartment, after all. I'm the guest. And I think we're both ready to turn in for the night."

He turned back to Marie. "Don't forget your promise."

She nodded. "I'm working on it. Have a good night!"

His eyes lingered over Kathy for another second before he turned to the door and stepped into the hall.

"Thanks for stopping by!" Marie called in a tone that seemed unnatural.

Kathy waited several seconds after Credan had left to ask her mother, "Who was that?"

Marie waved it off, not meeting her daughter's eyes. "Oh, he was just a friend."

"That's funny."

"What's that, dear?"

"I mean, you've been dead for twenty years. I didn't think your social life would spring back up so soon. After all, as far as your *friends* are concerned, you're dead."

Marie's mouth stretched open in a yawn. "Oh my! I'm so tired!"

"Me too. That's why I don't have the patience for the run-around."

Her mother's head snapped up to meet hers. "Excuse me?"

"I want to know if that man—" She pointed toward the door for emphasis. "—has anything to do with your sudden reappearance."

Marie began to shake her head, but Kathy's tone stopped her in her tracks.

"Don't lie to me, Mom. I have a right to know. And so does Samantha. *Especially* Samantha, who has a family to worry about now."

The older witch let out a heavy breath and dropped her head. "Yes, Credan is involved with my reappearance."

"How, exactly? Is he another witch? A sorcerer? A wizard?"

Marie remained tight lipped until another yawn struck her—a real one this time, from what Kathy could tell. "I really am tired, dear. Can we talk about this in the morning? Besides, I'd rather hear about your date. It must've gone well if you were out so late." She looked at the clock. "It's nearly midnight."

Kathy was in no mood to chitchat about her date, but she also didn't want whatever short time she had with her mother to be ruined by her accusations. Not until she talked to Samantha and they could put up a united front to demand answers.

"It was fine." She had intended to leave it at that and then decided to throw in a curve ball. "Actually, we spent most of the time talking to a witch whose partner was just murdered."

Marie's face dropped, which was exactly what Kathy had intended. "Who was it?"

"A woman named Cassandra. She and her partner own an occult shop Samantha and I go to a lot for ingredients for potions and rituals and such. Oh, and Cassandra's partner is the one who married Samantha and Steven."

"And she was killed? How?"

Kathy shrugged. "Not sure yet. But it was right outside her shop. And there was only one witness, who claimed that there was no fight or anything. The man who approached her just lifted his hand to her heart and then she crumpled to the ground. So I'm guessing that it's related to magic in some way."

Marie reached behind her for the barstool at the kitchen island and sank into it.

Kathy left her mother sitting there and disappeared into the bathroom to get ready for bed. She didn't want to tarnish this second chance at getting to know her mother, but she also couldn't just stand by and let Marie blow them off when they deserved answers. If there was one thing she learned as a witch, it was that secrets only hurt you.

After she had washed her face and brushed her teeth, Kathy emerged from the bathroom, where Marie had made up her bed on the couch.

NECROMANCER

In the darkness, Kathy couldn't tell if her mother was awake still, but there was something she needed to get off her chest anyway.

"I don't like all of these secrets you're keeping. That's not what we do in this family and it's ruining our reunion."

CHAPTER 16

Ryan jumped up from the table and greeted Kathy with a hug when she and Marie stepped into the kitchen at Samantha and Steven's house the next morning.

"Good morning," he said against her ear. When they parted, he added, "And happy birthday."

She smiled bashfully.

Samantha groaned from where she stood near the coffee pot.

"Happy birthday," Steven echoed.

Marie rushed over to where Josh sat in his bouncer in the corner by the table. "There's my boy!"

Steven and Samantha exchanged looks, but nobody besides Kathy seemed to notice. Ryan retook his seat, sandwiching

Marie between Steven and Ryan, although her focus was on the baby.

"Samantha?" Kathy said. "Can I talk to you for a second?"

The sisters stepped into the next room. Immediately, Samantha said, "I'm sorry for what happened in there when you and Ryan saw each other. It's just still so weird to me that—"

Kathy shook her head. "Sam, I'm not worried about that. Not right now at least."

"Then what is it?"

"Ryan and I went to talk to Talia last night."

Samantha's eyes grew wide. "Kathy, you didn't! I specifically told you to stay out of it!"

"And I didn't think that was a good idea."

She scoffed and started pacing around the foyer.

"Look, I'm glad I went," Kathy went on. "Talia was shattered."

"Well yeah."

"And she had no one. Worse, everyone has been treating her like she and Cassandra didn't mean anything to each other. She's getting no information and she's being treated terribly by the police and the hospital staff."

Samantha stopped pacing and crossed her arms. "How is she doing?"

"As well as can be expected, although she's frustrated on top of it all because nobody is giving her any updates about

Cassandra since they weren't technically married and they're relationship was…unconventional."

"That's horrible."

"I know. She was so relieved when she saw me."

Samantha sighed. "Okay. So maybe you *were* right to go see her. But next time maybe call me first? So that I can join you."

"It was kind of a spur of the moment thing. Actually, it was Ryan's idea."

"If he was with you, how much did he hear?"

Kathy shook her head. "Nothing that he shouldn't have heard. We really only talked about Cassandra. Her death is supernatural, Sam."

"How do you figure?"

"Just the way that she died. Based on what Talia overheard from a witness, the guy who approached Cassandra didn't even touch her. And yet she was dead."

Samantha narrowed her eyes. "I'm not convinced."

"Well, either way, I think we should look into it to be sure. We owe that to them. They're our friends."

The older sister looked down at the floor. "Yeah, they are."

"Anyway, there's something else I need to tell you. Something weird that happened last night with Mom."

"She seemed fine last night when she was here."

"Maybe, but the man I saw her talking to in my apartment when I came home was a little suspicious."

"What man?" Samantha asked.

"She called him 'Credan,' and she admitted that he had something to do with her reappearance, but I couldn't get anything else out of her about it."

"How is he related to her reappearance, exactly?"

"Oh, *there* you two are!" Marie said as she emerged from the kitchen. "Samantha, dear, the creamer that you had out is gone. Do you have any extra?"

"It should be in the fridge." Samantha kept her body facing Kathy, indicating that they weren't finished with their conversation and should be left alone.

"That's what I figured, but I couldn't find it."

Samantha rolled her eyes and crossed the house into the kitchen, all the while mumbling about her husband not being able to "look past his nose."

Kathy followed and stepped into the kitchen just as Samantha pulled out a full carton of creamer.

"It's right here, Mom." She looked around her to Steven. "You couldn't have gotten it for her?"

Steven held Josh in his arms and was feeding him a bottle. "That's where I said it was!"

A realization came over Samantha and she turned to her mother for an explanation.

"Oh, I must've missed it," she said. "Thank you for your help finding it."

Kathy took a seat and eyed her mother as she fussed around the kitchen. She knew finding the creamer was just an excuse.

Marie didn't like it that Kathy and her sister were having a private conversation. Samantha didn't like that their mother had secrets.

CHAPTER 17

Nothing. There was nothing in the magic book about Credan, nor was there any mention of him anywhere. Kathy had even searched the book for anything else that might explain her mother's sudden reappearance, but so far had come up empty.

Typically, if someone was raised from the dead, either their soul was twisted and deformed, depending on how long they'd been dead, or their body was so far decomposed that it would've been obvious that the were no longer among the living.

Kathy's mother, on the other hand, looked as though she had simply disappeared in 1970 and reappeared at their doorstep in 1990. Kathy couldn't find any source of magic that would explain that.

"There you are." Samantha quietly pushed open the door into her bedroom and joined her sister on the floor beside the bed. With the baby monitor in hand, it was obvious that she had just gotten Josh down for his morning nap. "What are you doing in here?"

Kathy shifted awkwardly on the floor, and dropped her eyes to the magic book.

"Is this about Mom?"

She shrugged.

"Do you want to tell me what's really going on?"

The younger sister sighed. "I guess I sort of have…mixed feelings about Mom. On one hand, I'm happy that I finally get to know her. But on the other, I can't help but be very suspicious of her and the real reason she's here. She hasn't been giving us straight answers, and I don't like it."

Samantha rested her head back against the edge of the mattress. "Neither do I. But she's here now. And I want to take that opportunity to show Mom everything that we've accomplished. Everything that she's missed."

"But doesn't it all make you think about Dad too?"

Samantha reared back. "How so?"

"I mean, if Mom could find a way back from the *dead*, why couldn't he find his way back from wherever he is?"

"I don't know. Honestly, there's a lot about our own parents that we don't know. I mean, what was Dad really going through for him to run off an abandon us like that? He's probably out there somewhere, with a brand new life, ignoring our calls. Maybe he's even relinquished his powers too, so we can't track him."

"Is that really what you think happened to him?"

Samantha was quiet. She stared at the floor for a moment before she admitted, "I'm really not sure. But sometimes it's easier to think that. It gives some sort of explanation for why he's not here and why we can't reach him."

"But you think it's his choice that he's not here," Kathy pushed.

"I don't know. I mean, Mom found a way back. Why hasn't he?"

"Mom found a way back after *twenty years*! Dad's only been gone for six years."

"And that makes it better?"

"Maybe." Kathy shrugged. "All I know is that Dad loved us. I'm certain he still does. I can't believe that he'd just go and run off unexpectedly."

"Well. Whatever happened with Dad—and whatever is going on now with Mom—we're not going to figure it out by sitting here and wondering." Samantha used the bed behind her to help her to her feet, but Kathy remained where she was. "What is it?"

"It's just that, I can't help but think about Cassandra's death. I have this feeling that it's somehow all related."

Samantha crossed her arms. Kathy could tell she was

skeptical, but she didn't voice any objections.

"I know that you think it's none of our business, but even you have to admit that it seems awfully coincidental. I mean, our mother suddenly shows up from the dead without an explanation, and the same day a witch dies?"

The older witch sighed. "When you put it like that…" She studied her sister. "You're not going to let this go, are you?"

"No. I'm not. This is our job as witches."

"Is this really how you want to spend your birthday?"

"Helping shine a light on a friend's murder? Of course."

Samantha watched her sister for a moment longer, then let out a deep breath. "All right. We can go to the medical examiner's office and check it out."

Kathy tossed the book aside and sprung to her feet. "Thank you!" She wrapped Samantha in a hug. "This will be so much easier with your help!"

The older sister pulled away. "No part of this will be easy. But we'll go check out the body. I'll use my power to get some answers out of the doctor to find out how she died and what exactly we're dealing with, and then we'll go from there."

Kathy nodded. "Yeah, we'll definitely need your power. But wait, isn't the medical examiner in Pittsburgh? That's, like, two hours away."

"You said this was how you wanted to spend your birthday," Samantha said. "Besides, spending a few hours in the car with you isn't the worst way to spend the last few days of my maternity leave. I'm going to have to get used to the idea of leaving Josh anyway."

Kathy pulled her sister in for another hug. "Thank you for doing this."

"Yep. That's what I'm here for." She pushed her away. "Now get off of me. I have to go tell Steven that he's on dad duty today."

CHAPTER 18

Samantha and Kathy went back into the kitchen, and the older witch sidled up to her husband, who was finishing up the dishes in the sink. Ryan wasn't around and Marie was sitting at the kitchen table, finishing her coffee.

"Thanks for doing those," she said. "I was going to get to them later."

Steven shrugged. "It's no big deal. Now you can relax today instead. I figured you'd want to hang out with your mom and your sister."

"Actually…" Samantha glanced over at her mother, who took note of her tone and looked up. "Kathy and I were thinking of taking the day and going down to Pittsburgh."

"Pittsburgh?" Steven dried his hands with a towel. "What's there?"

Samantha shot her husband a look. Her mind was scrambling for an explanation that wouldn't raise her mother's suspicion.

"We've actually been planning a trip to this one spa for a few weeks now," Kathy said. "I guess Samantha just forgot about it with Josh and all. And then, of course, Ryan's visit. And Mom's."

"Yeah, we've been meaning to do it ever since Josh was born," Samantha added. "Before, actually. We were hoping to go before the baby came as a sort of last hurrah before I became a mom. Then, of course, he came a little early."

Steven smiled. "He had his own schedule."

"Anyway, we thought Kathy's birthday was the perfect time to do it." It amazed Samantha how naturally the lie came. She felt bad about it, even though she knew she'd explain it all to her husband later. He would understand, of course, but the ease of the lie still caught Samantha by surprise.

Steven didn't seem to catch on to the lie in the moment, though. He leaned in close to his wife and murmured, "But don't you want to spend time with your mother?"

Marie shot up from the table and approached the island, where they had all congregated. "I don't mind. I love the fact that the girls are still such best friends."

Samantha caught her sister's eye and smiled. *That* wasn't a lie.

"And Steven, if you want to spend time with your cousin, I

could stay here and watch Josh," Marie suggested. "Oh, I'd feel like such a *grandma*!"

"Uh…well…" Steven hesitated and looked to his wife for help.

Ryan came back into the kitchen, freshly showered and ready for the day. "Hello again, everybody. Steven, what time did you want to get going?"

"Where are you two going?" Samantha asked.

"I was hoping to show Ryan around town," Steven explained. "Maybe stop in at my parents' and my grandpa's so he can say hi. I know my mom's been dying to see him." His eyes darted up to Marie, instant regret on his face. "Unless we brought Josh to my mother's—"

Samantha shook her head. "I don't think that's necessary."

Mary, Steven's mother, had had a weird reaction to Josh. She loved to play up the role of Grandma when it suited her. But when it came to relying on her to watch Josh or feed him or change his diaper whenever they went to visit, Mary always had an excuse to pass him off to her husband or anyone else nearby. Samantha respected the fact that Mary was Josh's grandma, but she didn't like the idea of leaving Josh in her care all day.

Ryan looked around at everyone. "I take it we're not going out today?"

"I forgot that Samantha and Kathy were going to Pittsburgh today for Kathy's birthday," Steven said. "So we need to stay here with Josh."

"Nonsense!" Marie said. "I told you, I could watch him."

"That's a big ask, Mom," Kathy said. "I haven't even watched Josh on my own for longer than a couple hours."

Samantha nodded. "She's right. Josh can be finicky sometimes, and I really want to keep him on a schedule as much as possible."

Marie rolled her eyes and smiled. "You girls act like I didn't raise the two of you! Josh is a baby, and I know babies."

"Um, actually," Ryan cut in. "I'm a little tired from staying up so late last night. If it's okay with you, Steven, maybe we could just hang out here. Especially if we're going to have a party here later." Clearly, he had picked up on the tension.

"Right!" Kathy blurted. "Mom, you need to get this place ready for the party."

"Didn't you say you wanted to bake a cake?" Samantha asked.

"I could do that while he's napping," Marie said. "Besides, he can sit in his bouncer and watch me while I get the house ready. I used to do that with you girls all the time."

"Wouldn't it be better if all three of you went to Pittsburgh?" Ryan suggested, looking at the girls.

Samantha's eyebrows rose. "Um…well…"

"We'd love to have you, Mom," Kathy said. "But it's just that we've already booked a two-person spa reservation down there. If we had known you were coming…"

"Yeah and they were pretty expensive," Samantha added.

"So I'd hate to see it go to waste." She saw concern in her husband's eyes at the word "expensive." Another thing she'd have to explain later.

"Besides, we'll see you later," Kathy said. "You probably want to relax after your long trip, Mom. Where is it you came from again?"

"A lot farther than Pittsburgh." Marie turned back to the kitchen table and sipped the last of her coffee. "If you girls are going to make it to your reservations in time, you should get going." She brought her cup over to the sink.

Steven glanced down at it.

"Oh, don't worry about it," she told him. "If I'm going to spend the day cooking for this party, I'll be creating a lot more dirty dishes than that. I'll do them later. After all, I'll have all day."

Samantha could hear the hurt in her mother's voice, which pained her, but at the same time, they couldn't risk Marie coming and asking questions about why they were at the medical examiner's office and not a spa.

"Mom's right." Kathy stepped over to Ryan and gave him a hug. "Have fun here today. I'll see you later?"

"Wouldn't miss it."

Samantha kissed her husband. "Josh should sleep for another hour or so. He'll probably want his second nap around two, but don't let him sleep much longer than four. Otherwise, he won't go to bed at his usual time, which means his feedings tonight will be off."

He nodded. "Yes, dear. I know. How long do you think you'll be?"

Samantha glanced at her sister, then turned back to her husband. "Hopefully we'll be back here in no time, feeling refreshed and relaxed."

He kissed her again. "Hopefully."

CHAPTER 19

Samantha felt a headache coming on from the magical mind games she'd been playing all morning. Ordinarily, using her power didn't tire her out, but she'd been out of practice since becoming a mother, and the people she'd been persuading all morning to allow her and Kathy entry into the medical examiner's office were all smart, educated people, which took more energy to sway their minds.

"I actually just finished the autopsy," Dr. Morris said as she led them down the hall. Where the front lobby had been welcoming, almost warm with the soft chairs, art on the walls, and plants in the windows, the back part of the Allegheny County Medical Examiner's Office—the part that most people never saw—was much more stark. Sterile, even. The only things that decorated the walls were fire alarms and maps of the facility, leading people to the exit in case of an emergency.

"Were there any surprises?" Samantha asked. She needed to do all of the talking. If Kathy spoke up, there was a chance that Dr. Morris would've broken out of the magical manipulation that Samantha was putting her under.

"Um…sort of." Dr. Morris opened the door to her office and held it open with her back as the sisters walked in. "I still have to do my final report, so there are some things I want to look into, but I can give you the initial findings." She booted up her computer, then dug through the pile of file folders on her desk. "Please don't take any of my initial findings as key pieces of evidence just yet. I will submit my full report as soon as I can."

Samantha nodded. "Of course. We just want to get a general idea of what we're dealing with."

The story she had fed the unsuspecting doctor was that she and Kathy were police detectives working on the case pertaining to Cassandra's death. Samantha's persuasion forced Dr. Morris to not even question them or their credentials—or their casual springtime attire.

"Here's her file." Dr. Morris set a folder on top and pulled a sheet from inside it with her field notes. "Where would you like to start?"

"I suppose the beginning is as good a place as any," Samantha said. "When was Cassan—the *victim*—brought in?"

It was difficult for her to not use Cassandra's name, but if she was going to pull off her ruse as a detective, she needed to sound like one.

"Yesterday." Dr. Morris scanned the paper in her hands. "Looks like she arrived here around four o'clock, although the Erie County Coroner had pronounced her dead at ten thirty in the morning."

Samantha looked over at Kathy, who nodded. The story lined up with what Talia had told her.

"Was there any attempt to revive her at the scene?" Samantha asked.

Dr. Morris shrugged, but then glanced down at the report. "Oh, I see here. There was no pulse upon arrival of the police, but an initial attempt at CPR was made regardless. After several minutes and still no pulse, they determined she was too far gone."

Samantha dropped her head down, trying not to picture the scene. Still, she couldn't help but imagine Talia crying as swarms of people surrounded Cassandra to help her and slowly gave up on resuscitating her. It must've been completely heartbreaking.

"What were the findings of the autopsy?" Samantha fought to keep all emotion from her voice. It was funny how she'd been more prone to crying since she'd had Josh. She blamed it on hormones, but she suspected it might've been a shifted perspective of the world thanks to motherhood.

Dr. Morris sat back in her chair. "There were no physical signs of an attack or anything. No abrasions, cuts, scrapes, or anything."

"Anything internal?"

"It's hard to say until I get the tests back from the lab. There could be a number of things that had gone wrong internally, but as far as I can tell, her heart just stopped beating."

The sisters exchanged glances again. Without exchanging words, they both confirmed their suspicions: this attack had been supernatural.

"I'm almost positive the lab results will show something, though," Dr. Morris went on. "A young, healthy girl like that doesn't just drop dead unless something else is going on. Something she likely wasn't aware of—or maybe didn't tell anyone—but people don't just die of natural causes while walking on the sidewalk. Not without other signs showing up first."

"You don't think it could've been a heart attack or anything?" Samantha needed to rule out all possibilities.

"Not that I can tell." Dr. Morris shook her head. "Like I said, once I get the results back from the lab, I'll know more. But my best guess?" She rested her chin on her fingers as she thought. Finally, she let out a breath. "I couldn't tell you. I'm sorry. Based on the medical records I've received from her GP, she was perfectly healthy. No underlying conditions noted or suspected. Of course, something could've been going on that she didn't know about, or that the doctors never picked up on, but I think it's unlikely. As far as I can tell, she was healthy."

"And now she's dead," Kathy said.

Dr. Morris stared at her, confusion floating across her vision.

Samantha stood. "Thank you for your time, Dr. Morris." She reached her hand across the table. "I very much appreciate it."

The doctor shook each of their hands. "Of course. I'd love to help out in any way I can. Do you need me to walk you out?"

"I think we can get it," Samantha said with a smile. "Thanks again."

They waited until the door to Dr. Morris's office closed behind them in the hall before they started on their discussion.

"Did you hear what time Cassandra was pronounced dead?" Kathy asked. "That was only an *hour* after Mom first showed up at our doorstep."

"We don't know for sure that this has anything to do with Mom." Samantha pushed through the door into the lobby. They both smiled politely at the receptionist, who had taken quite a while to convince to let them talk to Dr. Morris.

Out in the April sunshine, they once again talked freely.

"I think Cassandra, Mom, and that Credan guy are all related," Kathy said.

Samantha tucked her hair behind her ears and crossed her arms. The medical examiner's office was on a narrow, rather quiet, street. "I'm not willing to jump to that conclusion yet.

Let's give Mom the benefit of the doubt."

"We need to question her," Kathy insisted. "Force her to tell us what she's keeping from us."

Samantha looked beyond her sister, down the street where one lone car had turned in their direction. "No. We need to talk to the police first."

CHAPTER 20

The weather was unseasonably warm for April. The temperature was forecasted to hit the mid-seventies by two o'clock. At the moment, the thermostat sat comfortably at sixty-five, allowing Steven to take his young son out in the backyard, where he and Ryan sat in lawn chairs.

Josh smiled and giggled as he watched the birds fly overhead, the squirrels try to get to the bird feeder, and the wind softly moving through the trees.

"Sorry we couldn't go out today," Steven said.

"It's okay. Honestly, I'm just as grateful for a quiet, relaxing day."

Steven took a sip of his second cup of coffee for the day. "It is nice out, isn't it?"

"Yeah." Ryan chewed on his thumb. "There is one thing that's been bugging me."

"What's that?"

"Why didn't Samantha want her mother watching Josh?"

"Picked up on that, did you?"

"Hard not to."

Steven sighed. How would he explain the behavior without exposing Samantha as a witch? "Well…Samantha and her sister have a lot of…unresolved issues with their mother."

Ryan nodded. "Ah. Is that because she was gone for so long?"

"Exactly. They just have some stuff to work out. And it doesn't help that today will be the longest time that Samantha's ever been away from Josh. Leaving him with his father instead of her estranged mother just felt better for her."

"That makes perfect sense."

Steven took another sip of his coffee, relieved that Ryan bought his excuse.

The back door swung open. "It is much too cold out here for little Josh! Here, let me take him inside so he can warm up. He can help Grandma bake Aunt Kathy's cake!"

Steven looked down at his son. He wore a long-sleeve onesie, pants, a hat, and a tiny little jacket. His lower half was covered in a blanket. Moments before, Steven had been wondering if he was *too* warm.

"He's fine," he told Marie.

"Trust me on this." She walked up to Josh and unbuckled him from the stroller. "I'm a mother."

Steven shot to his feet. "And I'm his *father*." He nudged his way between Marie and Josh. "I think I know what's best for my son." He held the back of his hand to his son's cheek, which was about the only part of him exposed. "I think he's a little warm, actually. See for yourself."

Marie held her hand to her grandson, then sighed. "Well, I suppose so. But with all of these bugs and dirt and who-knows-what floating through the air, it can't be good for him!"

"The fresh air?" Ryan asked.

Steven rebuckled his son in the stroller. "Don't worry. I've been watching him. When he starts to look uncomfortable, I'll take him inside." He pulled off the blanket and tossed it over the handle of the stroller. "There. Is that better, bub?"

Marie crossed her arms. "I was hoping to take him to the grocery store to get some supplies for Kathy's party. The more he gets out now, the more he'll learn how to behave in public later."

"I think he's comfortable where he is," Ryan said. "Look, he was just smiling and laughing."

Steven leaned in closer to Marie and murmured, "How would you even pay for anything at the store?"

Marie held his gaze, but didn't have an answer for him.

With another sigh, Steven pulled his wallet out of his back pocket and handed Marie fifty dollars. "Here. Take this and get what you need for the party. You can even take my car."

"I don't—" She stopped when she saw that both men had made up their minds. "Okay. I suppose I'll be right back then."

CHAPTER 21

When Marie returned to the kitchen after her failed attempt to get Josh alone, she saw Credan standing at the island waiting for her. Her eyes grew wide and she grabbed his arm and pulled him out of the room and away from the windows that looked into the backyard.

"What on *earth* are you doing?" she hissed.

Credan smiled as she held his arm, and when she noticed, she instantly released it.

He tugged at his clothing, as if to regain his composure. "Are you any closer to securing the child for me?"

Marie put one hand on her hip and the other rubbed her forehead. "I'm working on it."

"Work faster," he said harshly. "I need the child."

She pulled away and looked at some of the pictures on the walls. Samantha had already filled the frames with images of the newest member of the family.

Credan picked up on her mood and stepped toward her. "I'm sorry, my love." He tried to wrap his arms around her, but she shrugged him off.

Marie took a step away from him, but when she turned and saw his face, she said, "We need to keep up pretenses if I'm going to pull this off. Kathy saw you at her apartment. Right now, I think they suspect *you* to be the enemy. Which means that if you and I are seen talking—"

"They'll suspect you as well." Credan nodded. "I understand. You are brilliant, sweetheart."

She resisted the urge to roll her eyes. "There's something else I need to ask you. Something that's been…bothering me."

"What is it, dear? Anything. You can tell me anything."

"That witch who died. Kathy's friend…was that you? Are you the one who killed her?"

Credan pulled away and paced the front foyer. "I don't know what to say. I don't want you to change your impression of me."

Too late for that, she thought. "It was you, wasn't it?" she asked.

Slowly, he nodded.

"How could you? She was innocent! She wasn't doing anything!" She noted her voice raising and immediately stopped further outrage.

"How could *I*? I warned you, my love. I told you that each day you spent with your daughters would come with a price."

"Someone else's *life* is the price? If I would've known that, I would've—"

"Made the same choice," Credan said plainly. "We both know it. You would've given *anything* to see your daughters again, even if you knew the consequences. So you can't blame me for killing her when I told you your second chance at life would come with a price. I'm not the one who ended your life early. You did. It's not my fault you didn't like the consequences, but that was the choice that you made twenty years ago when you killed yourself. And it's because I love you that I gave you a second chance at life, but even that comes with a price until you deliver on your promise to me."

Marie stared at the floor. She couldn't meet his eyes. She couldn't say anything, for risk of completely melting into her emotions. He was right. She *had* ended her own life too early. Even if she had been manipulated. Now, she was using magic to fight the natural order of the world and give herself a second life, which would require the sacrifice—or multiple sacrifices— of other people who ordinarily were meant to live long happy lives.

"Hurry up and get me that baby," Credan said. "I'm growing impatient."

CHAPTER 22

"I'm starving." Kathy bit into her sub and wiped the mayo from the corners of her mouth as she chewed.

They had stopped for lunch at a small café on Chestnut Street in Pittsburgh, across the Allegheny River from the where they had visited the medical examiner's office.

"Me too." Samantha picked at the pieces of her own sub that had fallen from the sandwich. "I guess I didn't think about how long we'd be gone."

Kathy glanced at the clock on the wall. Just before noon. They hadn't been with the medical examiner for long. It had taken more time to drive the two hours down from Erie than it took them to ask about Cassandra's death.

"So." Kathy pressed her lips against her wrist in an attempt to cover her mouth as she swallowed her last bite. "What are your thoughts on what we learned today?"

Samantha held up her sandwich, but her eyes drifted to the counter where the barista was wiping down the countertops. "I don't know, Kathy. I just feel like we're digging around *trying* to find some kind of supernatural connection to Cassandra's death. Like Dr. Morris said today, she'll know more when she gets some lab results back. Maybe we should just wait until then."

Kathy was shaking her head before her sister even finished talking. "No. I'm telling you, Sam, someone is trying to pull the wool over our eyes. I don't think it's *necessarily* Mom. It could be someone using her as a pawn. Her reappearance alone is enough suspicion to be skeptical. It just seems like a distraction."

The older sister shrugged and nodded. There was no arguing with that logic. In a quiet voice, she asked, "Do you think it was stupid of me to leave Josh alone with her?"

"He's not alone. He's with Steven. And Ryan."

"But they don't have powers and, as far as I know, Mom does. I just don't know what they are, and that kind of scares me."

"It's astral projection." Kathy popped a piece of turkey in her mouth casually. "It's not lethal or anything, so you can relax about that."

Samantha sat up straighter, surprised. "How do you know what her powers are?"

"Dad told me."

"When?"

"A long time ago."

"Oh." Samantha took a sip of her drink. "Did you and Dad talk about Mom a lot?"

Kathy shrugged as she chewed. "Often enough. Up until recently, I've never really had any memories of her. Dad was willing to answer any questions I had. I guess it helped me develop some kind of connection to her, beyond old pictures."

"I guess I never knew that."

They were both quiet. Kathy took the last bite of her sandwich and then reached for a napkin to wipe her hands. "I know I never *truly* knew her, but based on the stories that Dad told, the woman who's back seems different from the stories he used to tell me."

"Well, it's been just about six years since Dad's been gone, so those stories aren't exactly fresh in your mind," Samantha said. "Besides, memories and reality are two different things. Dad was her husband and, from what *I* know of their marriage, he adored her. His opinion—and his view of her—was biased. Not to mention, the way Dad just up and disappeared, he clearly had secrets of his own."

"When are you going to let this grudge against Dad go?"

"He abandoned us, Kathy. Left us to barely scrape by. Need I remind you of how we both had to work seven-day weeks just so we could keep the house?"

"No, I remember that very well, actually. But that just proves my point, Dad didn't just adore Mom, he adored us too.

He wouldn't abandon us and leave us with the mess that he did. Not intentionally, at least."

Samantha remembered the conversation she'd had with her mother the night before. Where Marie had told her that she would never willingly abandon them. Samantha wanted to believe her father felt the same way, but it was hard to argue with the facts that she knew to be true: one day he was there, then he was gone without a trace.

She cleared her throat. "You can believe what you want, Kathy. All I know is that if Dad wanted to see us—if he loved us enough—then he would find a way to come back to us. After all, Mom did."

Kathy balled up the wrapper from her sub in her hand. "And look what kind of secrets she's come back with."

CHAPTER 23

Marie rushed outside at the first sound of her grandson crying. He lay in the stroller, where Steven was rocking it back and forth to try to get him to go to sleep.

"I think he must be hungry." Marie rushed up and pulled Josh out of the stroller and onto her shoulder. "I'll go get him a bottle. I just finished up the cake and I need to take a break before I start on the dishes. You two relax. I'll take care of everything."

She barely cast Ryan a pacing glance as she hurried to get Josh inside.

"Actually," Steven said as he rose, "I'm getting a little hungry myself. It's just about noon, so why don't we all eat?"

Marie stopped by the back door and offered a toothy smile.

Her insides knotted with worry. "That sounds great!"

She hurried inside and peered through the kitchen window. Steven and Ryan were finishing up their conversation and slowly folding up the lawn chairs. Now was her chance.

Pressing Josh tightly to her, she raced up the stairs, recalling faint memories of performing the same action over twenty years ago with her own children. It brought back a feeling of nostalgia that she wasn't expecting.

Up in the nursery, Marie closed the door behind her and pressed her back against it. She let out a deep breath, hoping to dispel the aching sense of regret that had been building in her the longer she spent with her newly-expanded family. Nothing could erase the terrible feeling in the pit of her stomach, but she pushed it away.

She crossed the room and considered setting Josh in his crib until she could summon Credan, but she thought better of it. If anything were to go awry, or if she were to change her mind, she wanted Josh in her arms so she could protect him.

Across the rivers and the seas.
Hiding out where spirits be.
I call the one who raised me.
Bring him here, I summon—

The door burst open when Stephen emerged and interrupted her spell.

"What's going on in here?" There was accusation all over his face, but he didn't voice it.

Marie locked eyes with him for only a fraction of a second before she turned and set Josh on the changing table. "His diaper was wet. I thought I'd change him before I fed him his bottle." She glanced over her shoulder and saw Steven's shoulders lower as he relaxed from whatever confrontation he was gearing up to pursue.

"Oh."

She reached from the drawer and pulled out a fresh diaper. "Have you and Ryan decided what you want for lunch? Eat lightly. We'll have a lot of food tonight when the girls return."

"No, we haven't." He stepped forward and nudged Marie aside. "Here, I can do that. Why don't you go downstairs and relax? You've been working all morning."

Marie sighed. "If you say so. I was just trying to spend some time with my grandson."

Steven put one hand on Josh's belly to keep him on the table as he turned and looked at his mother-in-law. "Uh…well…this will only take a second."

She nodded. "Right. I understand. I'm overstepping. I'm Grandma now, not Mom. I'll go down and find us something for lunch."

As she walked out of the room, she felt frustration that Steven had interrupted her spell and that she'd need to find another way to have a few minutes alone with Josh to make the trade.

A bigger part of her, however, felt relief that she had been interrupted. The growing sense of guilt was eating away at her and, if Credan's plan was successful, the sacrifice was something she wasn't sure she could live with.

CHAPTER 24

It was late-afternoon by the time Samantha and Kathy made it back to Erie. They found a spot to park on South Park Row downtown and then walked up to the police station.

Thanks to Samantha's persuasion power, they were being escorted back by a frizzy-haired blonde receptionist, who very easily succumbed to Samantha's power, to the open office that the Erie Police Detectives all shared.

"Detective Paulson will be able to assist you with what you're looking for," she told the girls when she deposited them in front of a messy desk with two chairs across it.

The seat at the desk was empty, but the receptionist had already returned to her post at the front desk—anxious to get back to her crossword puzzle, Samantha assumed.

Kathy took a seat in one of the chairs and Samantha followed.

"So what's our plan here?" Kathy leaned in close and whispered to her sister.

Samantha glanced around at the other detectives, one who seemed to be eyeing them every few seconds. He looked familiar to Samantha somehow. She wondered if her father knew him from when he worked in the same building years ago when he worked for the city's Public Works department.

Turning to her sister, she whispered, "We ask this detective his version of events. See how the match up with the M.E.'s version and what we know about Mom and that guy she was talking to."

"Credan."

Samantha nodded. "Right. And keep quiet this time. When you started talking with Dr. Morris you broke my connection with her and she almost clammed up. It's better if we operate like you're not here."

Kathy mimed locking her lips. "I'm the silent partner. Got it."

The man across the room was staring at them now. Samantha caught his eye, but immediately looked away. If he recognized them, using her persuasion would be harder. She would be splitting her focus between two men, who were both trained to weed through lies and deception.

The man pushed away from his desk, looking as if he was

about to get up and cross the room to them. Samantha tensed at his movement, but relaxed when another man stepped toward them with a steaming cup of coffee.

"Oh, I'm sorry," he said. "I didn't realize you were waiting." He set his coffee down on his desk. He had blond hair and kind eyes, a look that seemed to contrast his profession.

Samantha smiled at him. "That's okay. We weren't waiting long."

He offered his hand to each of them. "I'm Detective Paulson. How can I help you?"

"Well…" she started, but her eyes trailed over to the other detective, who had returned to his paperwork, but was very clearly still listening. Turning back to Detective Paulson, she pushed her power through her voice when she asked, "Is there somewhere more private we can talk?"

Immediately, he nodded. "Mm-hmm. Follow me." He rose and led them through another door that opened into a long, stark, all-business hallway. They stepped into the first room on the right, which seemed to be the break room. There were two circular tables with chairs around it, a couch against one wall, and three vending machines against another. Along the third wall was a kitchenette of sorts, with a short countertop, sink, and a microwave. Next to that sat a refrigerator.

"This is perfect," Samantha said. She took a seat beside her sister at one of the circular tables.

"What is it I can help you with?"

Once again, she laced her words with persuasion. "Will you please tell us all you know about the death outside Mystic Treasures yesterday? A young woman died."

Detective Paulson was somber. "Yes, that was very unfortunate. However, I have to admit that it isn't much of a case, really. There's not much to go on."

"What *do* you have?"

He ran a hand over his stubbly chin. "Honestly, the only reason we suspect foul play is because of a witness statement. Apparently someone who lives across the street saw her and another man outside her shop. According to his statement, the two of them seemed to be arguing before she fell."

"Arguing about what?"

Detective Paulson shrugged. "I don't know. It's really just the one statement that makes that claim, so I still need to check into it. If it wasn't for that, we would've just assumed she had a heart attack or some other medical emergency. We haven't received the report from the M.E.'s office yet, so we can't be sure."

"But she was young and healthy," Samantha said. "You really think it was a natural death?"

He shrugged. "I don't know. I'm not a doctor. We'll have to see what the autopsy report says."

"So is the man that she was arguing with a suspect?"

"He's certainly a person of interest," Paulson admitted. "But until we talk to him and get his side of the story, and gather some other details from yesterday morning, we can't really pinpoint *who* is a suspect yet."

Samantha nodded. "That makes sense." She looked over at Kathy, signaling *dead-end* through her eyes.

"Can you describe the man that was arguing with her?" Kathy asked.

Now, Samantha shot daggers at her sister with her eyes.

Detective Paulson stammered, his eyes switching between the two of them.

There was a knock on the door and then it opened. The man who had been eyeing them in the open office stuck his head in. "Mike. We need to go. There's been another woman killed. Same thing as yesterday. Broad daylight. Out on the street. No blood. No obvious sign of attack. Young and healthy."

"And now she's dead," Paulson finished.

The other man nodded.

"Okay, I'll be there in a sec. Let me finish up here."

The man gave the sisters another look before closing the door.

"Sorry," Paulson said to the girls. "I'm afraid I'll have to cut this short. Was there anything else I could help you with?"

Kathy shook her head no, but Samantha spoke up. "Who was that man? The one who popped his head in?"

The detective looked back at the door for a second before returning to Samantha. "Him? That was Detective Hillman.

Gary Hillman. Do you know him?"

"Not really," Samantha said. Recognition finally set in. "He was a friend of our father's. But that was a long time ago."

CHAPTER 25

Samantha pulled up the car on Payne Avenue, right behind the patrol car that they had followed from the police station downtown. As they got out of the car, it wasn't hard to miss the large garage facing East Lake Road that was painted from top to bottom graffiti-style. Upon closer inspection, it was advertising a tattoo parlor facing East Lake Road.

On the sidewalk, the sisters saw the white sheet covering the victim's body. The area was swarming with police officers. Several were interviewing witnesses, another group was looking around the area where the body lay, and another officer was rolling out police tape.

"We got here just in time." Kathy nodded toward the officer sectioning off the area.

"Not soon enough, though," Samantha murmured.

"Let's split up and see what we can find out." Kathy started toward one of the officers interviewing a witness.

The witness was an older woman, with a threadbare sweater pulled tightly around her. Her midsection was round, but her legs were pencil-thin. She wore worn, pink slippers and white pants. Her thinning blonde hair was peppered with gray.

Kathy tried to look as if she were meant to be there, so she mimed the detectives canvassing the area for clues.

The trouble was, East Lake Road had been widened so much that it was essentially a highway now, and the cars raced by at top speed, making it difficult to hear.

"…minding her own business, just walking down the…" A car whizzed by, blocking out the end of her sentence. "He just walked up to her and she looked a little scared, but didn't run or nothing."

"What did the man look like?" the detective asked.

"Tall. Broad shoulders. A bit…sickly-looking, I guess."

"Hair color?"

There was silence. Kathy had her back turned, so she assumed the woman shrugged, or gestured in some other way that she wasn't sure.

"What happened after he approached her?"

"I couldn't hear because of…" Another car passed, illustrating the words that were inaudible. "They didn't look friendly to each other, though. Next thing I knew, the girl was falling to the ground and the man was walking off like nothing happened."

Kathy let out a deep breath. She spent another few minutes looking around while the detective asked the witness some personal questions about how to contact her for further information. After she let enough time pass, she returned to her sister's side.

"Anything?" Samantha asked.

"Sounds like it was the same kind of attack that happened to Cassandra," Kathy said. "Non-existent to the naked eye."

"So supernatural?"

"That's what it sounds like. And, judging by the statement of that woman over there," she nodded to the woman who was crossing the street back to her house, "the guy who attacked this girl sounds *a lot* like Credan."

"Does it *actually* sound like him, or do you just *want* it to?"

Kathy looked her sister in the eyes. "You need to trust me on this one, okay? I know you're hesitant, but my gut is telling me that something's going on here. Something to do with Mom."

Samantha sighed. "Okay. So what are we going to do about it?"

"I think we need to question Mom. We can't let her get away without an explanation."

"I don't know, Kathy," she groaned. "I know it's the best course of action, but I don't want to destroy the relationship with her when she only just returned to us."

"Okay. I get that. But if she's involved in some bad stuff, then that means she needs our help." Kathy held up a finger as she leaned in to her sister. "Not to mention, she's supposed to be dead. The fact that she's suddenly alive again is unnatural, even for us, who are very well-versed in the *super*natural."

"I know. I get what you're saying. Like I said, I know it's the right choice, but…" She shook her head. "I just hate it."

Kathy nodded. "So do I. But I would rather miss her memories and wonder what it would've been like for her to have never died, than for her to come back unnaturally and tarnish whatever precious memories we *do* have of her. Especially if she's continuing to lie to us about it."

"Yeah."

Kathy watched as the police continued to scour the scene of the crime. "So…are we going to talk to her?"

Samantha nodded. "Yeah. But *after* your party tonight."

"Are you sure that's a good idea? That man could kill—"

The older sister put up her hand to stop her. "I think we can wait. The murders seem to happen every morning—if they're even connected. If we question Mom right after the party, then that will probably be before the next murder takes place."

"Are you willing to risk someone's life on a *probably*?"

Samantha crossed her arms. Her face was unreadable. "If we're about to ruin whatever renewed relationship we have with her, then I think we deserve some normal experiences with her too." She turned to her sister with tears in her eyes. "*You* deserve to celebrate a birthday with her that you actually remember."

Kathy breathed in a deep breath. She was still nervous about the idea of waiting, but she knew there was no arguing with her sister. Besides, it *would* be nice to spend a birthday with her mom. "Okay. We'll wait until after the party."

CHAPTER 26

Steven squeezed his wife tightly after the sisters arrived back home later that afternoon. "I'm so glad you're back."

"Did you miss me?" Samantha pulled away. "Or was Josh giving you a hard time?"

"Josh was an angel!" Marie cheered. "He's still taking his afternoon nap. Should be up soon."

"I'm just glad that we can leave the house now," Steven said.

"Actually," Ryan piped up from Kathy's side. He still had his arm hooked around her after he had welcomed her home with his own hug. "I was hoping the birthday girl could show me around town."

Steven's shoulders slumped. "I guess so."

"No, it's okay," Kathy said. "I don't want to ruin your plans.

We've already ruined them enough today."

Ryan turned to her. "But I was hoping to spend time with you. Alone."

Samantha groaned. Kathy shot her a look.

"Actually, I think it'd be perfect if you and Ryan go out on a quick little date," Marie said. "There are some things I still need to finish up for the party later. Decorations to put up. Gifts to wrap."

"What kind of party are you throwing?" Samantha asked. "I didn't think this would be a full soiree."

"Only the best for my little girl," Marie beamed. "Two hours would be perfect. Oh, and try not to eat anything while you're gone. We'll have *plenty* of food."

"Well…" Kathy looked to Steven for approval.

"Go ahead," he said. "I suppose he'll be here until Friday anyway. We'll have time to do stuff."

Kathy and Ryan headed back out to the car, where she got behind the driver's seat.

"You're not letting me drive today?" Ryan pulled on his seatbelt.

"If you're going to get a tour of Erie, then your guide needs to be an Erie native." She backed out of the driveway, turning her body to see out the back window.

"So where are we headed?" Ryan asked as they approached the intersection at Cherry Street.

"If it's all the same to you, I'd rather go somewhere to stretch my legs," she said. "I've been in the car for most of the day, so I'm a little restless. Plus, if Mom doesn't want us to eat, then that kind of limits us."

"Do you have any ideas?"

She smirked at him before returning her eyes to the road. "I'm a native, remember?"

Fifteen minutes later, they were getting out of the car at Frontier Park. The sun was fading, casting golden rays across the green space. Kathy tried to push away the memory of the trickster she and Samantha had defeated in the same park just last summer.

Ryan reached for her hand as they walked along the winding pathway. "This is a beautiful place."

Kathy nodded. "I like it. It's a little bit of a drive for us, but I like the open spaces and all the flowers."

"Can I tell you a secret?"

"Have we reached the secret-sharing part of our relationship?"

"It's a small one."

"Go on."

"I really just wanted some time alone with you."

She snickered. "That has to be the worst-kept secret in history. I think it was pretty obvious. You even said so yourself."

"I like spending time with you, Kathy."

"I like spending time with you too." Although, even as the words left her lips, she wasn't thinking about Ryan nearly as much as she was thinking about her mother and Cassandra and Credan and that other woman who was killed. How did they all fit together? What was her mother hiding? She and Samantha had agreed to wait until after the party to question their mother, but she wasn't sure she could wait that long. She needed answers.

"So tell me a little bit more about yourself," he said. "I know this is sort of like our second or third date, but I feel like we haven't had very conventional dates so far."

"Sorry about that."

"It's okay. I'm still intrigued by you, so it's not all bad."

She gestured to an empty bench overlooking Cascade Creek running through the center of the park. "Why don't we sit and talk?"

As they approached the bench, Kathy rubbed her hands up her arms and shivered. "Should've worn a coat. It was warm today, but with the sun going down…"

Immediately, Ryan pulled off his own coat. "Here. Take mine." He draped it around her shoulders before she sat.

"Thanks. That's better."

They listened to the water stream through the creek. Watched as the wind gently pushed the budding branches around the top of the trees. It was peaceful. Restful. Just what Kathy needed. This moment made her birthday perfect.

"You're quiet," Ryan said. "Is it your mother?"

Kathy smiled. "You're perceptive."

"Do you want to talk about it?"

"Maybe."

"Do you mind if I ask: what's the story behind that? I mean, Steven said that your mother had passed away, but then yesterday you said that it just *felt* like she passed away." He shrugged. "I don't understand. If she skipped out on you guys, why did you even let her in the door? And the way Steven reacted to her today, it was like he didn't want her alone with Josh, which I guess I understand if she *did* leave you years ago. But then you all seem like a perfect happy family in front of her." He sighed. "I guess I'm confused. And now I'm bombarding you with questions when *you* had something on your mind. I'm sorry."

Kathy smiled softly and shook her head. She knew this conversation was coming eventually. And she was glad that Ryan had been such a good sport about the lack of information up until now. "No, it's okay. You don't have to be sorry. It is a weird situation. The truth is, I never grew up with my mother. But I've always wanted to know her."

"Well, yeah. Naturally."

"My dad raised me and Samantha, all on his own. He loved my mother so much that he talked about how great she was. And then when she showed up at our doorstep, I guess we just wanted to get to know her ourselves, finally. But now that I am getting to know her, I guess I'm…" She paused as she searched for the right word.

"Disappointed?"

Kathy shook her head. "No. Not really. I mean, I knew that my father had these rose-colored glasses when it came to my mother, so I wasn't expecting the saint he made her out to be." She looked down at her hands. "I don't know. I guess I'm just sad for the time I missed with her."

"Like, you wished she was there your whole life?"

"Something like that. I'm an adult now. I'm grown. I've created a life without her in it. I needed her when I was a child, a teenager. But that moment has passed and we'll never get it back. I've grown up without a mother and now I don't need one."

Ryan let out a sigh and then put his arm around her shoulders and pulled her in close. He kissed the top of her head.

Kathy leaned into him, letting him console her. She wasn't crying. She wasn't sad. She wasn't sure exactly how she felt. But it was something. And having him hold her, without saying anything, was exactly what she needed. It was exactly what she wanted.

CHAPTER 27

Kathy sat at the dinner table and tried her hardest to enjoy herself. The party was for her, after all. Everyone had gathered to celebrate her birthday—her mother had spent the whole day cooking a delicious meal and baking way more sweets than she needed to.

And yet, Kathy couldn't get her mind off of everything she and Samantha had learned from their field trip to Pittsburgh earlier.

Josh began to whimper in his high chair between Kathy and Samantha.

"You can't be hungry," Samantha murmured. "I fed you a full bottle before we sat down."

"Maybe it's a growth spurt," Steven suggested.

"Or maybe he needs to burp," Ryan added.

"Or maybe—" Kathy reached over and pulled Josh out of his high chair and into her lap. "—he just wants to see his Aunt Kathy on her birthday." She bounced him on her legs and made faces at him, which distracted him from his crying.

"So, Ryan," Marie started, "what do you think about Erie, after Kathy's tour?"

"Well, we really just went to Frontier Park," Ryan explained.

Steven reached for another cookie from the plate in the center of the table. He scoffed. "I would've showed you more places than *that*."

Ryan ignored his cousin. "Erie has grit, but there's definitely a certain charm to it."

"Up here must be very different from what you're used to down in North Carolina," Samantha said.

"It is. But I also wouldn't be opposed to moving up here."

"Why would you do that?" Steven asked.

"For Kathy."

The room fell silent as everyone exchanged glances.

Josh's crying broke the tension.

"Maybe it's his bedtime," Marie suggested.

"Did you say you'd move to Erie for *Kathy*?" Samantha blurted. She caught her sister's confused look, then added, "That didn't come out the way I intended it. It's just…you two have only known each other a short while."

Marie came around the table to Kathy's side. "Here, let Grandma put you to bed."

"Did I hear you right?" Steven asked. "You want to move up here?"

"For Kathy," Samantha added. "Let's not forget the part where he said he'd move across the country for a girl he just met."

Ryan shrugged. "I like her."

Kathy's mind was racing. She passed her mother Josh and then leaned forward on the table. What kind of messages had she been sending him? Did she ever indicate that he *should* move for her?

Josh's wailing subsided as Marie took him upstairs. In the silence that followed, Ryan said, "It's obviously too soon to say for sure, but if things between me and Kathy go the way they've been—if they get more serious—then, yeah, I would consider moving up here. I mean, it's not like I don't have family up here too. It wouldn't *just* be for Kathy."

"I'm flattered." Kathy took a sip of her drink to try to cool herself down. Suddenly, she felt very hot. "But Ryan, we've only known each other two days."

"*Two days!*" Samantha echoed.

Kathy held out her hand to quiet her sister. "I didn't think you'd be planning our future already. You barely know me. Besides, isn't this something we should've discussed privately before you brought it up at a family dinner?"

"I know, the timing is terrible," Ryan admitted. "And yes, I know we haven't known each other for long, and we're still getting to know each other, but—" He reached across the table for her hands. "—I know what's in my heart. And it's telling me that I'm falling in love with you."

Out of the corner of her eye, Kathy could see Samantha rolling hers. Kathy pulled her hands away from his.

"Ryan, listen, I like you—I like talking to you—but I'm not looking for anything serious. I thought the two of us would just have some fun this week, and then it'd be done when you go back to North Carolina."

"I am having fun. I just thought…" Ryan looked defeated.

"I'm sorry." Kathy hated seeing the hurt on his face.

Steven shot up from his chair. "Come on, Ryan. Let's go into the sunroom and talk it over."

With some encouragement, Ryan rose and followed his cousin out of the dining room.

In their absence, Samantha sighed and reached for her glass of water. "Well, I was *not* expecting *that*."

"Me neither."

"I didn't realize you were leaving such an impression on him." Samantha shrugged. "Then again, I'm not surprised. You always leave a mark on the boys."

"Sam, this is serious!" Kathy snapped. "Ryan is upset."

"Kathy, you didn't do anything wrong. You wanted to have some fun with him, you did, and now he's heading down the aisle."

"Actually, it hasn't been as much fun as I thought it'd be," the younger sister admitted.

"Why not?"

"Because of…" Her words trailed off and she met Samantha's eyes. In unison, they said, "Mom."

The next moment, they both jumped up from the table and raced for the stairs.

CHAPTER 28

Marie considered Credan's proposal. How her life would be so much different if she had been alive. How her daughters' lives would be different. Sure, Credan had said that they were doing well, but was she really about to take his word for it? That wasn't nearly enough to satisfy her desire as a mother, to see her children successful and living happy, healthy lives.

If what he said was true, and one of her girls was a mother now, that meant that Marie had already missed out of her grandchild's birth. Her daughter's pregnancy, likely even her wedding. Marie had already missed their childhoods. They had been stolen from her after the manipulation of that evil witch, Morta.

Marie felt her maternal instincts recharge. The same ones that had been repressed after twenty years in obscurity. She had missed a lot of her daughters' lives, but if there was a chance for her to return to them, to see her grandchild and be a part of their lives, then she needed to take it. No matter the costs.

"What do you need my help with?" she asked Credan carefully. She didn't want to seem too eager, although she could tell that he knew he had her hooked.

"It's no secret that I love you," he said. "I want to be with you. To hold you. Cherish you. But in order to do that, you need to be brought back to life."

"And you have the power to do that?"

"Indeed, I do."

"So that makes you…a necromancer?"

He nodded. "It's how I've been able to pull your soul from the billions of others suffering in this God-forsaken place."

She shook her head. "Then you shouldn't need any help bringing me back to life."

Credan held a finger in the air. "Ah, but I do. You see, I have the power to bring someone back temporarily, but after a few days, I tire. My magic gives out and the soul is suddenly ripped from reality and dropped back to wherever it is that they came from. And, trust me, it's as painful as it sounds."

Marie winced, imagining the pain of suddenly being pulled away from her girls, after finally being reunited with them.

"Now, if you wanted to be brought back *permanently*," he

went on, "that would require more power. Youth. And the only way to obtain enough power to grant someone in death a renewed eternal life is to take the youth of a child. The younger the better."

Marie's eyes widened as she realized what Credan was getting at. "You want my grandchild."

Credan was kind enough to try to offer a sad smile, although his true apathy shone through. "Yes, I do. It's the only way to ensure you'll be mine forever. That you'll be with your daughters for the rest of their lives. And only *you* can help with that."

She shook her head. "My daughters would never go for that."

"Of course not. That's why you'd need to trick them." He sensed her hesitation and added, "You see, my thinking is that you'll need to do it quickly. They'll be so overjoyed that you're back that they'll be practically *throwing* the child at you. You'll just have to take one of those moments to slip out, bring the child to me, and I'll do what needs to be done."

"And what am I supposed to say to them when they ask me where the baby has gone?"

He waved it off, like it was a trivial thought. "You'll figure something out. Frame it as if you don't know. Send them on a wild goose chase for some demon that doesn't exist. After a while they'll give up looking."

Marie knew that wasn't true. As a mother, she knew that she

never stopped thinking about her daughters. Samantha and Kathy, whichever one was now a mother, would never be able to forget about their child. Especially if they had been kidnapped.

As much as Marie knew that she would never be able to give her grandchild to Credan, she also knew that she needed to get back to her daughters, even temporarily. Once she was back with them, maybe they could figure out a way to make her second life permanent. At least, make her second life last as long as her natural life should have.

"What are the conditions?" she asked.

Credan smiled. "That's what I love about you, darling. You're able to see the bigger picture. You truly are brilliant."

She raised her eyebrows. "The conditions?" It took every effort not to tell him off. But, he was right about one thing, she needed him.

"Since I'll be the one to raise you from the dead, I will maintain some level of control over you."

"Control? What kind of control?"

"You'll still have free will, of course," he said. "But I can make certain things…*off-limits*, if you will."

"As in…?"

"You're forbidden from warning your daughters—or anyone else—about our plan to give you a second life. You cannot tell them a single thing, in any way, or insinuate that things aren't how you make it seem."

Lying to her daughters wouldn't be easy, but it was a small

price to pay to see them again. Of course, without their help, she would have a harder time finding a way to get out from under Credan's control, but once she was alive again, she'd have access to *The Art of Magic*, which would put her in touch with all of her ancestors' knowledge of magic and the supernatural. Surely, there would be something to assist her in freeing herself from Credan and allowing her to stay alive with her daughters.

"I can do that," she said. "When will you—"

"And," he went on, "each day you spend with your daughters that you *don't* deliver their baby to me will come with a price."

"What kind of price?"

"You'll learn of it when the time comes."

Marie took a deep breath as she searched his face for anything else that he might be hiding or keeping from her. The offer was risky, but if it meant reuniting her family—if only even part of it—then she was willing to take that risk.

"If you don't succeed in handing me the baby," he said, "then I will take your soul instead. My love for you is immense, darling, but my survival instincts are stronger. Bringing you back from the dead will take an awful lot of magic that will be difficult for me to maintain. If you fail, I will be forced to use the power radiating from your soul to help replenish my strength."

"Would my soul be enough? How do I know you won't just go after the baby once you've taken my soul?"

Credan shrugged. "If you're gone, my love, there will be no reason to go after the baby. I will simply be recouping my losses on a bad investment by taking your beautiful soul."

Marie resisted the urge to roll her eyes. These were not the words of a man in love.

"You may not be a youthful baby, but your power will go a long way in helping me regain my control over the dead."

"So you benefit either way."

"If you succeed, darling, we'll *both* benefit."

Not if I can help it, she thought to herself.

"Now that you've heard my terms, what do you say? Do we have a deal?" He held out his hand to her.

Marie considered it for a short while. Despite the risks, there was not a doubt in her mind that she would do anything to see her daughters again.

She shook his hand. "Deal."

CHAPTER 29

"Anything?" Samantha asked when Kathy came down from the attic.

"No." Kathy shook her head with a solemn expression. "Just the same old boxes that have been up there for years."

Samantha tucked her hair behind her ears and paced the floor. The hardwoods creaked under the weight of each step. "I never should've left him alone with her. I was just so distracted by what Ryan said. I'm a terrible mother."

Kathy gripped her sister by the shoulders. "Stop. You're an amazing mother. It's *our* mother who isn't doing so hot right now."

"Where do you think she's taken him?"

"If I had to venture a guess, I'd say somewhere with Credan."

"And we know nothing about him." Samantha balled up her hands into fists. "When we find her, I'm going to kill her."

"She's already dead," Kathy said. "Besides, that attitude is not going to help us get Josh back. We need to be smart. Mom has obviously taken him somewhere, but I don't know if she necessarily wants to hurt him."

"How do you know, Kathy? She's been lying to us this whole time! Just like you said she was!"

"Right, but when has she ever shown any kind of negative emotion toward Josh? She loves him, despite what she's done. I think there's a chance that we could save him from whatever she's planning if we find her in time to make her feel guilty about what she's about to do to her grandson. Speak to the mother inside *her*, and hopefully she'll do the right thing."

"And how do we find her?"

"With magic," Kathy said. "Get started on a spell to find him."

Samantha shook her head. "I can't focus right now. The spell wouldn't work. Besides, you're better at writing them than I am."

"But you're his mother. You have a stronger connection to him than anyone else. The strongest, I would argue. Use that connection to find him."

Samantha let out a deep breath and nodded. "Okay. What

are you going to do?"

"I'm going to forewarn your husband about what we're doing," Kathy said.

"I don't want him knowing. He's going to freak out."

"*You're* freaking out. Steven is Josh's father. He deserves to know, no matter how he reacts. And, no offense, but you're not the best person to tell him right now. Not while you're panicking. That's only going to make Steven freak out too."

"Okay."

"Now get started on that spell."

As Kathy made her way downstairs, she suddenly realized that her heart was racing. She had been so busy trying to manage Samantha's emotions, that she never took into account how she was feeling about it herself.

But there wasn't time for that. Whatever her mother had planned, they needed to act fast.

In the sunroom, Steven and Ryan were seated in the wicker furniture against the windows. Neither of them noticed her approach.

She cleared her throat.

"Kathy!" Ryan rushed up to her with his arms stretched out.

Quietly, she put up a hand and shook her head. Whatever was going on between them needed to wait. "I was hoping to speak to Steven. Alone."

Ryan looked between the two of them, then nodded and left the room without another word.

Kathy closed the door behind him.

"You're going to have to give him something to go on sooner than later," Steven said. "Break up with him if you're not into it, because right now he feels a little like you're leading him on."

"I know. But that's not what I wanted to talk to you about."

His eyes searched hers for answers. "What is it? What's wrong? Is it a demon or something?"

"It's Josh. He's missing."

Steven's eyes grew large. "Missing? How did this happen?"

"We think our mother has him," Kathy said. "That's the working theory, at least."

He ran his hands over his face. "Oh my God. I have to—you have to—we have to find him." He started in one direction, then moved in a different direction, before stopping in front of Kathy again.

"We will," Kathy assured him. "Samantha is working on a spell to find him right now. The best thing you can do is to stay here in case our mother returns with him."

"And do what when she comes? I don't have any powers."

"No, but you're a parent. Convince her to hand him over to you, where he belongs. I'm sure we wouldn't be far behind if she *does* end up back here. Now, I need to go find your son." She turned to leave, but Steven caught her arm.

"Kathy! What's going on? Your mother being back, the trip you and your sister took today. I've been in on the secret long enough to know that you two are working on something."

"Last night, when I got back to my apartment, I saw my mother talking to some strange man." The idea of calling her mother "Mom" while she had kidnapped her nephew was out of the realm of possibility in Kathy's mind. It was easier to refer to her simply as "my mother." "And then two witches have died since she's been back, one of them being the partner of the woman who married you and Samantha."

"Oh." Steven took a step backward.

"Yeah, so that's where we went today, to see how it was all connected. We wanted to interrogate our mother after dinner today, but obviously that didn't go as planned."

"So you still have no idea where he is."

"We'll get him back," Kathy promised. "You just need to trust us." She leaned in and gave him a quick hug. She turned toward the door, but stopped and looked back at him. "You and Ryan *really* do look alike."

CHAPTER 30

Samantha was hunched over a book in the center of her bed when Kathy stepped through the door. She had a notepad with scribbles on it in her lap, pencil still poised in her hand.

"What's all this?" Kathy asked.

"Well, I've been thinking about everything since you've been gone."

"You mean, in the ten minutes that I was downstairs?"

Samantha noted the attempt to lighten the mood, but didn't comment on it. They had more pressing matters to deal with. "I want to be prepared for whatever we're about to walk into. I mean, if the spell I came up with works and we cast a spell to take us to Mom, there's a good chance it'll also take us to the person who helped bring her back from the dead—we know that much for certain."

"Right, but I couldn't find anything about any of that in the magic book."

"But I *did* find something in a mythology encyclopedia we had up here." Samantha tapped a book to her right. "There's an entry on necormancers."

"Necromancers?" Kathy came over and took a seat beside her sister to read the book.

"They have the ability to raise the dead," Samantha said. "By stealing life forces from other beings. The younger the sacrifice, the longer the resurrected will live."

"You think Mom is trying to sacrifice Josh to regain her life?"

Samantha let out a deep breath. "I hope not, but it's the best theory I've come up with."

Kathy rubbed her sister's back and then leaned her head on her shoulder. "I don't think Mom would do that."

"You said it yourself. We don't really know her."

The two were quiet for a moment, both of them lost in their thoughts.

"So who do you think the necromancer is?" Kathy asked. "Credan?"

"I'm certain he is. And not only would Josh's youth bring Mom back for good, but it would also strengthen Credan as well."

"But why would he need more power?"

"Why do any of them need more power?" Samantha asked. "It's greed, not need."

"But that can't be his only goal," Kathy said. "I mean, obviously our mother would want to be resurrected, but why would Credan agree to help her with it? Just because he can, doesn't mean he will. She has to be doing something for him, and if he needs to use most of Josh's youth to give Mom a long life, then there isn't much left for Credan to profit on."

Samantha uncrossed her legs and got up. She hated talking about her four-month-old son like he was currency. Especially at the hands of her mother. "I don't know, and frankly I don't really care. Knowing that Credan is a necromancer means that I know how to kill him."

"Did you come up with a spell?"

She ripped off the top sheet from her notepad. "It's right here. I'm just working on the final spell to send us to Josh."

Kathy held up a finger and turned to the magic book, which lay open on the bed. "I think I may be able to modify one that's in here."

"Hurry up. I hate thinking about what Josh might be going through without me."

CHAPTER 31

Marie clutched Josh tight to her chest, even as he wailed at the top of his lungs. With her other attempts to summon Credan having been interrupted, Marie opted to meet him somewhere else instead. This time, they chose an old warehouse by the lake that had recently been abandoned.

"The faster you hand over the child, the sooner you can have your life back." Credan held his arms out for the baby. "And the sooner that thing will *shut up*!"

Marie rocked Josh to try to console him, but she knew he would sense her nerves—the tension within her—that nothing would soothe him.

Even a four-month-old child didn't trust her.

"Is it going to hurt him?" she asked over the sound of Josh's crying.

"Ripping his life force away from him? How do you *think* it will feel?" He inched closer. "Now is not the time to develop an attachment to the little brat!"

Marie felt the familiar pang in her heart at someone criticizing her child. Only, Josh wasn't her child. But she still felt the close connection to him. Is this what it felt like to be a grandparent?

"You *promise* this will give me a long, healthy, natural life?" she asked.

Credan barked out a laugh. "My dear sweetheart, there is nothing *natural* about the life you're living now. Yes, by taking the child's life force, you will get a second chance at life, but it will hardly be *natural*. Your natural life ended twenty years ago at your hands!"

"But you're a necromancer. You can make anything possible. And you've already killed two people. Witches, on top of it. Isn't their combined life forces enough to give to me and maintain my life? Why do we need to harm a child?"

Josh continued to scream, making his discomfort known and ratcheting up the stress of the conversation.

"Because I need the power from their life forces for myself," Credan said. "Their deaths gave *me* the power to make *you* alive again, but the life force from this child will be the one to truly restore your life."

Marie felt tears prickle her eyes. She looked down at Josh as she continued to rock. His face was red and he had tears running down from his eyes. Her heart ached with the thought of this poor child being harmed. But she would miss her own children if she didn't retain this second chance at life. She hated the consequences, but if that meant more time with her daughters, more time pursuing the dreams that she threw away when she mistakenly took her own life all those years ago, then maybe the sacrifice was worth it.

Still, her body refused to obey and she simply stood there and smiled down at her inconsolable grandson with her own tears.

"Give me the child!" Credan demanded. "Or I will rip him from your arms!"

"Don't you dare!" Samantha shouted from across the warehouse.

Marie turned and saw her daughters charging toward them. Relief flooded through her. The choice was no longer hers to make, now that her daughters were intervening. Maybe Credan could find another way. One that wouldn't mean sacrificing her only grandchild.

Kathy put up her hands in an attempt to use her magic, but nothing happened.

Credan turned on them and sneered. "I'm immune to your powers. Something to do with toeing the line between life and death."

"Fair enough." Kathy picked up an errant piece of pipe laying on the ground and swung it at Credan's head. It collided with his skull making a loud smacking sound. "But you're not immune to *that*."

Marie clutched Josh closer and took a step back while Kathy took another swing at Credan. Samantha, however, was on her and trying to pull Josh away from her.

"Sam, I'm so sorry." Marie held Josh closer, pulling him away from his mother's hands. She knew she needed to hand him over. She knew it was the right thing to do. She knew she didn't want anything to happen to the little boy that she had grown to love so immensely over the last couple of days.

But the thought of handing over her only hope at a renewed life was harder for her to do than she imagined. Even as her daughter frantically tried to take possession of her son.

"Give him to me!" Samantha demanded.

Marie took a step backward and looked down at Josh, new tears forming in her eyes. "He really is beautiful, Samantha. You did such a great job."

Josh noticed his mother and turned and reached for her, wailing even harder for her.

"Please, give him to me," Samantha said. "Don't hurt him."

"I would never—" But Marie stopped herself before she could lie. Yes, she had every intention of hurting him. Not directly herself, but by handing him over to a man who was essentially going to kill him for her own benefit.

NECROMANCER

"Mom—" Samantha's words were cut off when they heard a grunt escape from Kathy's lips and the metal pipe clatter to the floor.

Turning, they saw that Credan had her knocked flat on the ground. Blood spilled from his skull and he loomed over Kathy. The pipe she had been using to attack lay just out of her reach.

Slowly, he extended his hand out toward her, ready to use his power.

CHAPTER 32

Marie watched as both of her daughters struggled. Samantha looked back and forth between her and Kathy, while her younger daughter attempted to crawl backward on the dirty concrete floor, away from Credan. Meanwhile, Josh continued to cry in her arms.

"Now would be a good time for a little help here!" Kathy never took her eyes off of Credan while he loomed over her.

Samantha turned back to Marie. "Look what your greed has done to us! He's going to kill Kathy, and you're about to hand off your grandson to him!"

Marie stood frozen. She wanted to protect her family—but if she didn't let Credan take Josh, then she wouldn't be around to help them ever again.

Kathy backed up against the brick wall, loaded with cobwebs. "Guys! I've run out of rope here!"

Samantha watched as her sister struggled, then turned back to her mother. "Make a choice. Are you willing to let him kill your daughter, like you're willing to let him kill your grandson?"

Marie's body tensed up as she heard Josh wail in her arms—*He's not comfortable with me*, she thought—and saw the panic in both of her daughters' faces. The last time she had seen them, they were just toddlers. Babies themselves. Now, they were grown adults. Responsible, loyal, and *good*. And she was the one who brought pain and suffering to their lives. Something she never thought she'd bring them.

The next moment Marie knew, there were two of her. The second apparition appeared beside Credan. Apparently, even resurrected, she had her powers. Astral projection.

Astral Marie only took a second to make a choice. She pushed Credan to the floor, then extended her hand to help her daughter up.

Kathy refused to take her mother's hand and stood on her own. Astral Marie's shoulders sagged with disappointment, but she wasn't at all surprised.

Meanwhile, a few feet away, the original Marie handed Samantha her son. His whimpers began to subside as soon as he was back in his mother's arms and she began to rock and shush him.

Kathy returned to Samantha's side while the Astral Marie disappeared.

Shifting Josh to her hip, Samantha reached in her pocket and pulled out a piece of paper that she handed to Kathy. The younger sister held it out for both of them to read.

Stealing lives and killing spirits,
For your sins, you will be—

"You know," Credan said as he picked himself up from the floor, "if you finish that spell, the magic holding your mother to this world will cease to exist as well and you'll lose her too."

Samantha glared at her mother, then looked back to Credan. "Right now, that's a sacrifice I'm willing to make."

"Sam," Kathy said as a warning.

"She'll return to hell," Credan said. "Where she's been burning in eternal damnation for twenty years. You see, if it wasn't for me, that would be her fate."

Marie dropped her head, but she could feel her daughters' eyes on her.

"Mom?" Kathy asked quietly. "Is that true?"

She felt tears spring to her eyes, but she refused to wipe them away and show a sign of weakness in front of Credan. "It's true." She sucked in a shuddering breath. "It's because I committed suicide."

"Dad said you were murdered," Kathy said.

"That's what he believed to be true," Marie said. "Or rather, what he *wanted* to believe. He's the one who found me." She looked up at the both of them now. "But my suicide was not truly my choice. I was being targeted by an evil witch that I had stopped a week before my death. Her attack was subtle, but effective. Her curse got inside my mind. Made me believe that everyone was better off without me."

"Oh." Samantha's expression softened. "That's—"

"And then she convinced me to raise her from hell so that she could trade in your little boy and live again," Credan said.

Samantha's face hardened again.

"No, that's not exactly what—" But Marie's words were cut off by Samantha restarting the spell.

Stealing lives and killing spirits—

"Sam." Kathy put a hand on her sister's arm to stop her. "Are you sure you want to do that? Send our mother back to hell?"

Samantha glared at Marie. "Yes."

"Sam!"

"That woman—the one who was about to give away my baby boy to a *demon*—is no mother to me. It's because of her selfishness that two women are dead."

Now the tears flowed, and Marie didn't care if Credan saw. "I'm sorry. I'm so sorry! Samantha, I know what I wanted to do was horrible. Don't worry about me. Do what is right. I'll be okay."

She could see tears in younger daughter's eyes, but there was no sympathy in Samantha's. Kathy mouthed an apology before the sisters returned to the piece of paper and recited the spell.

Stealing lives and killing spirits,
For your sins, you will be punished.
From this world, you cease to dwell,
We banish you with this spell!

Credan began spinning in place as flames rose up around him and consumed him. As they intensified, so did his screams. His body began to spin faster and faster while the fire rose up around him. Marie could feel the heat lick at her skin and she raised an arm to shield her eyes. Another moment later, the necromancer exploded and sent a blast radiating throughout the warehouse.

Moments after Credan's demise, Marie felt the flames surround her. She let out an involuntary cry before the floor opened up beneath her and she was sucked back down to hell.

CHAPTER 33

The silence that followed the flames was nearly visible. Even Josh was quiet, as if he sensed that something had shifted. The tension was gone. Replaced now by a mixed bag of emotions that neither sister could even begin to sort out.

Kathy broke the silence by letting out a cry. She covered her mouth and sunk down into a crouching position as the tears flowed. Her eyes stared right at the scorch mark where her mother had been standing moments before.

"We need to find a payphone," Samantha said.

Kathy could hear the ache in her sister's voice. As much as she wanted to believe otherwise, even she wasn't immune to their mother's second death.

"We need to call Steven and let him know where we are so

he can pick us up." Josh began to fuss in her arms and she shushed him and began rocking him again. Still, his loud, innocent cries echoed throughout the spacious, empty warehouse.

Kathy rose and used the heels of her hands to wipe away her tears. She took in a deep breath, her chest still heaving with sadness, but she pushed it down. There would be time to fall apart later. When she was alone. By the look on Samantha's face, Kathy would have no company in her grief.

"I think there's an exit over here." The younger sister nodded to another corner of the cavernous space.

They found an overhead door. It had been graffitied and backed into by what looked like a large truck, so the door was misshapen with a large dent. It took Kathy some effort, but she managed to raise it enough for her to get underneath and hold her arms out for Samantha to pass Josh through before she crawled through herself.

Outside, they got their bearings. They were down on the waterfront. Across the Bayfront Parkway was Hamot Hospital. If they could get down to the intersection at State Street, they would be able to cross the busy highway and find a payphone inside the hospital.

"I know where we are." Samantha looked around. She didn't reach for Josh immediately and Kathy knew why. He was heavy, especially as he squirmed and wiggled around.

"Me too. This way."

They started down a forgotten road that was nearly on the water's edge. Kathy remembered from high school that this had once been the main industrial hub of Erie, which led to all of the commercial businesses on State Street. Products used to arrive on the boats and were then sold up the street.

Over time, the city has relied less and less on the industry along the waterfront until eventually, many of the factories along the lake closed up. Like the building they had just left, many of them had been left abandoned, if they hadn't already been torn down by the city.

"I didn't realize Mom had been burning in hell for twenty years," Kathy said quietly as they walked.

"Neither did I," Samantha admitted. "But after what she tried to do to Josh, she deserves to burn for a hundred more years."

Kathy knew that was mostly the anger talking for her sister. And Samantha had a right to be angry. But Marie was still their mother.

"We need to save her."

Samantha stopped in her tracks and put her hands on her hips. "Why? She's done nothing but bring us pain."

"Because she's our mother and, despite the things that she's done, we love her. Even if you can't admit that right now."

Samantha shook her head. "We don't even know her. Not really. All we know is what Dad told us about her. And look how much of a liar he turned out to be."

Kathy opened her mouth to fire another rebuttal, but Josh began to cry in her arms and she stopped. Samantha reached for him and hefted him onto her hip.

Quietly, they crossed the street and stepped into the main entrance for the hospital. They found the row of payphones near the main lobby and Samantha dug out change from her pocket. She struggled as she tried to count out the coins.

"Here, let me take him," Kathy offered.

"No." Samantha held him close. She managed to get the change into the slot and then dialed the house. "Steven? It's me. The bitch is dead. I have Josh. He's safe. Just scared." After another second, she said, "We're at the Hamot Hospital. Nobody is hurt, but this was the closest place we could find a phone. Swing around the main entrance and we'll watch for you."

After she hung up, the remaining change rolled into the slot and she dug it out and slipped it into her pocket. She hoisted Josh up higher. He leaned his head against his mother's shoulder, sleepy.

"You remember Mark? The guy we saved from the harpies?" Kathy asked as they made their way back to the lobby.

"Yeah, why do you ask?" Samantha slumped into a chair and shifted Josh so that he was laying against her chest.

"He was a terrible man." Kathy took the seat beside her sister. "You remember what he did to that girl?"

"What's your point?"

"He deserved to be punished, but not by burning in hell.

That was excessive. Instead, we made him confess to what he had done and let him go to jail for his crimes."

"Again I ask, what's your point? It's not like we can turn Mom into the authorities. What are we going to do? Tell them that a woman who's been dead for twenty years kidnapped my son and tried to turn him over to a necromancer?"

With it being so late, there wasn't anyone in the main lobby. Then again, after the evening's events, Kathy wasn't sure that a crowd would've stopped her sister from talking so freely.

"No, of course not," Kathy said. "What I'm saying is that Mom deserves the same grace."

"Where is this even coming from?" Samantha asked. "*You* were the one who was skeptical of her from the beginning."

"That's because I knew she was hiding something! Now that I know what that something is, and I know that everyone is safe, my views on it have changed. Because *Mom* is still not safe. She's burning in hell right now all because she committed suicide, something dark magic led her to do. Is that really her fault? Why should she be punished for it?"

Samantha looked at her sister's in the eyes. "Kathy, *drop it.*"

The younger sister rose and started to cross to the chairs on the other side of the room, but she stopped halfway and turned back to her sister. "If you want to be stubborn, then fine. I'll go down to hell *myself* and save our mother's soul because that's my duty as a witch, and as a daughter."

CHAPTER 34

"Tonight was weird," Ryan said as he and Kathy settled onto the couch in the living room.

Kathy had opened a bottle of wine and poured two glasses, which they both cradled, even though neither of them took a sip. "Yeah, it was."

"Are you sure Josh is okay?"

"I'm sure he'll be fine. He's tough." Since Steven had to pick them up at the hospital, the girls invented a story about Josh suddenly getting a very high fever and needing to go to the hospital. While they were there, they said, Marie had decided to take off again, without a trace.

It wasn't the best lie they had ever come up with to cover up their supernatural escapades, but it was enough for Ryan to buy into it and not ask too many questions.

"Sorry for ruining your birthday," he said.

Kathy scrunched her brow. "How did you ruin it?"

Out of all the things that had gone wrong today, Ryan didn't rank anywhere in Kathy's mind. Then again, there had been so much that happened that it was hard for her to keep straight. Her mind was fuzzy with exhaustion.

"By saying I would be willing to move up here…for you."

She nodded, suddenly remembering. That had felt like a lifetime ago. "Ah. Yes, I remember now." She took a sip of wine, but thought better of it and set it on the coffee table. The way this conversation was turning, she didn't need to cloud her judgement any further.

"I know I put you in an awkward spot and I didn't mean to make you feel uncomfortable," he said. "Especially not on your birthday. I wasn't trying to push you into anything. I just thought—"

She put up her hand to stop him. "Ryan. It's all right. You didn't ruin it. I got to spend time with the people I care about." She shrugged. "Granted, the ending wasn't great and I'm glad the day is over, but no, you didn't ruin it."

"Are you sure?"

Kathy's hand shot out to pat his arm, but she hesitated. She tried to recover and play it off, but he had noticed. "Don't worry about it."

Ryan glanced down at her hand, which now lay on the back

of the couch, then met her eyes again. "I'm going to ask you a question, and I would like you to be honest with me."

She shifted in her seat, suddenly feeling very hot. "Okay."

"Is there a future between us?"

Averting her eyes for a moment, she considered her response. It had been a while since she and Jeremy had broken up, but she still didn't quite feel ready to be with anyone else. There had been other guys along the way. Guys that she'd had fun with, including Ryan, but as far as having a future with one of them, Kathy couldn't see it.

"Honestly? I really don't think so." She made a face. "I'm sorry."

"No, it's okay. I told you to be honest."

"I like you, I really do. But I don't think there's enough between us to make a long-lasting relationship work."

Ryan was quiet, but he nodded while keeping his eyes away from hers.

"Besides," she said at an attempt at a joke, "Samantha doesn't like the idea of us together, and that alone is like the kiss of death."

He offered only a slight smile. "I think we could work on it, though."

She shook her head. "If it's something we have to work on this early in the game, then I think that's our sign that this isn't ever going to work out. And there's too much against us. You live in North Carolina, I live here in Erie. If you moved up here, like you suggested, and it didn't work out between us—or if we had a fight—you'd resent me and I'd feel bad for making you sacrifice so much. I don't want that hanging over our heads."

"I wouldn't feel like that, though."

"You don't know that for sure." She hooked an eyebrow. "Are you telling me that taking your boat on Lake Erie is the same as taking it out on the ocean?"

"Well…"

"Exactly. That's something you love, that you'd have to give up for me. Besides, you're Steven's cousin. There's already a family connection and that complicates things."

"Or it could make it so much easier."

"Maybe. But are you willing to risk everything else for that?"

He circled the rim of the wine glass with his finger. He still hadn't taken a sip yet.

"Thank you for being so supportive of me these last couple days," Kathy went on. "And for spending my birthday with me. You're a good listener. And you were here for me when I really needed it. I enjoy talking to you."

"I don't know if I want to go back to North Carolina, knowing that I'm leaving you behind."

"Well, it's a good thing you have almost another week for us to shift into a friends dynamic to help you adjust before you leave." She smiled. "I don't want you out of my life, Ryan. I just don't think we work together romantically. You're my brother-in-law's cousin. We're basically family."

He laughed. A genuine, heart-felt laugh. "Yeah. We're *so* closely related."

CHAPTER 35

Samantha couldn't stand the thought of being away from Josh for another second, so she had Steven move his crib into their bedroom before she laid him down to sleep. The poor child was so worn out from the evening's events that it didn't take much to get him to go down.

Even after he fell asleep, Samantha stood over his crib and watched him. Her heart swelled with love, while it simultaneously ached for what might've happened.

Steven came into the room and wrapped his wife in a hug from behind. "He asleep?"

She nodded. "Has been for a while."

He kissed her neck. "Good. I'm glad you're both okay."

"I'm sorry that I put our baby in danger."

"Don't. How could you expect that she was going to do that? You only saw your mother. Of course you immediately trusted her." He rubbed her arms. "How are you feeling after tonight?"

"I'm okay."

"Even thought your mother's gone?"

She looked at him, confused. On the way back home, she had been intentionally vague. Steven was nonmagical, so not only did he not fully understand all things magic, but he was often afraid of it all too. Especially now that there was Josh to consider.

"Kathy told me," he explained.

"Oh. Well, I'm glad my mother's dead. Again."

"That can't be true."

Samantha turned and glared at him, pulling away from his touch. "Don't tell me how to feel about this."

"I'm not. At least, I'm not trying to. All I know is that you've spent your whole life missing her, wondering what life could've been like if she had lived. These past few days, you've gotten to experience that and then, suddenly, it was ripped away from you. You're the most level-headed person I know, but I know that this has shaken you up. I know you're not glad that she's gone."

She sighed and sunk down onto the bed. She pulled her legs up to her chest and wrapped her arms around them. "I just can't get over the fact that she took Josh and almost handed him off to the necromancer."

Steven shook his head. "I don't think I need the details."

Again, she felt for her husband. In all of this magical mess, he truly was powerless. As a man, she knew that made him feel insignificant, which, of course, he wasn't.

"Is there any way to prevent him from being put in harm's way again?" He studied Josh as he asked.

"No. There isn't. Not until the bad guys learn that Josh doesn't have powers."

"And he never will."

Samantha swallowed down her guilt. The likelihood of Josh *never* developing his own magical powers was slim-to-none. Chances were, he was going to grow up to be a full-fledged witch like Samantha herself. Only, as far as Steven knew, that wasn't true. And at the moment, Samantha didn't want to start another argument. She was too tired from the day. Had too much on her mind.

"Apparently my mother's been burning in hell for twenty years."

That got Steven's attention, and successfully changed the subject. "She has?"

Samantha nodded. "Because she killed herself."

"Oh." He took a seat beside her.

"She was manipulated to do it all those years ago, but she still did it. And now her soul is paying the price for it."

"I guess that makes sense," he said. "In some religions, suicide is considered to be the worst sin, morally, that you can commit."

When Samantha didn't say anything to that, Steven asked, "Is that where your mother is now?"

"I think so. Kathy wants to go down to hell and retrieve her soul to free her, but I don't know if she deserves that. Not after what she did to Josh."

"Sam…"

"I mean it. If you had told me a week ago that she was burning in hell for something she had been pushed to do twenty years ago, then yes, I would've gone and tried to save her. But now? How can I forgive her for what she's done to our son?"

Steven breathed in a deep breath and wrapped his arms around his wife again. "Think of it this way: isn't the fact that she's missing out on her daughters' lives—and now her grandson's life—enough of a punishment? Why does her soul need to burn as well? Especially if it truly wasn't her choice to end her life."

Samantha considered his words, but the evening's events were a louder reel in her head, replaying over and over again. The sound of Josh screaming in her arms, her mother's hesitation to hand him over.

"I don't know. We're not going to figure this out tonight. I'm wiped." She stood and made her way around to her side of the bed. She climbed underneath the covers. The last thing she wanted was to go to sleep, knowing that her dreams would be filled with her mother, and what she had done. But if she had opted to stay up to do something to get her mind off of things, that would only worry Steven and make him think that she was fragile.

Steven leaned over and kissed her. "I love you." When she echoed his sentiment, he rolled over and turned out the light.

In the darkness, Samantha lay on her back and stared at the ceiling. The burning rage in the pit of her stomach didn't subside. There would be no getting to sleep tonight.

CHAPTER 36

Samantha wondered if it was wise to bring so many magical items with her to Kathy's apartment. The trunk full of candles, herbs, crystals, and other instruments rested at her feet, the smoky scent wafting down the hall. Meanwhile, she propped *The Art of Magic* against her waist while she waited for the door to open.

"Oh. Hi. Are you moving in?" Kathy asked when she answered the door.

"I came here to apologize."

The younger sister raised her eyebrows, but offered no other words. She simply stepped aside to allow Samantha to enter.

After pulling the trunk in behind her and resting it on the floor beside the coffee table, Samantha sat on the couch and set the book in front of her. Apologize first, cast spells later.

"Sorry for being so grouchy yesterday."

Kathy sunk down onto the opposite end of the couch and propped her head against her arm. "You could say that. What changed your mind?"

Samantha averted her eyes. "Honestly? I needed to separate my personal feelings from my responsibilities as a witch. If this were anyone else, I wouldn't let their soul burn in hell for a mistake they made twenty years ago."

"But this isn't anyone else. This is Mom."

"I know. And that's why I've been having a hard time with it."

"I understand that," Kathy admitted. "Especially after what she almost did to Josh. You were just worried for him, so *your* mother instincts kicked in."

"I guess so. I've been thinking about it all night and, while I can't forgive her for what she did to Josh, I also don't think it's fair to let her burn in hell for the rest of eternity. It's too excessive of a punishment. She's already been burning for twenty years. She deserves to move on."

"And," Kathy added, "it's possible that burning in hell for that long has warped her soul. You could argue that she never would've even considered trading Josh for a new life if she hadn't spent twenty years down there."

But she did offer him up, Samantha thought to herself, but kept those thoughts to herself. "Right."

"So now what do we do? Why did you bring all of that?" Kathy indicated the trunk and the magic book.

"That's why I'm here." Samantha set the book on the coffee table and began flipping through the pages. "I found this ritual in the book that I think will work to save her soul."

"How does it work?"

"It's supposed to transport us down to hell so we can retrieve her soul. At least, that's what I could gather from the spell." Samantha got up and opened the trunk. "But it's going to take some assistance."

The two sisters got to work setting up the ritual. Samantha had brought red candles from home, which she now pulled out and lit. Red represented, among other things, magic related to life that included spells relating to both birth and death. She also pulled out pennyroyal, myrrh, lavender, mandrake, and juniper to a large copper bowl. Kathy instinctively used a wooden spoon to mix the ground-up herbs together so they blended with one another. Samantha laid out an altar rug between the candles and Kathy set the bowl in the center of it.

The sisters sat on either side of the table and reached across it to join hands. The book lay on the side of the table, angled so they both could read the pages of the book. Together, they recited the spell aloud.

Blur the lines of the living and dead,
To the place where tears are shed.

NECROMANCER

Samantha felt her eyes grow heavy. The next thing she knew, her body was falling to the floor, but before she could feel the impact, her eyes opened and she was suddenly standing at the edge of a wide gray, hazy river. She stumbled a little at first, before she regained her footing. Magic had a way of disorienting you sometimes.

"Kathy!" Samantha called out, suddenly fearful that the spell had gone wrong. She spun in a circle, frantically searching for her sister. After spinning two more times, suddenly Kathy was beside her.

"Whoa. That was a weird spell."

Samantha hugged her quick and then pulled away. "I'm glad it worked. Now the question is, where are we?"

Kathy looked out at the river. "I'm not sure. Is this something from mythology?"

"The River Styx," Samantha said. "We need to find a way across it."

"Do we?" Kathy asked. "Or do you think we can call for her soul from here?"

"You think it's that easy?"

"Well, she was just sent back to hell last night," Kathy reasoned. "And Credan had pulled her soul from the eternal flames before, so maybe…" She shrugged.

"Okay, but then how?"

Again, Kathy shrugged.

The two of them looked at each other for a moment, and then turned toward the river and began shouting.

"Mom!"

"Marie!"

"Mother!"

"Marie Walker!"

Samantha stopped and listened as their echoes carried across the river. "It's not working. And now I feel like an idiot."

"Maybe it's not her name we need to call for. I mean, think about it, in all of human history, how many *Marie*'s or *Mom*'s have died?"

"True. But if we don't call for her name, then how are we supposed to call for her?"

Kathy thought about it. "Maybe we should be calling for her spirit. Connect to her soul on a human level that she can recognize instantly as her daughters. You know how like people with dementia might not remember their lives, but they can still feel the love of their kids and spouses?"

"But she isn't a dementia patient."

Kathy rolled her eyes. "I'm theorizing here, Sam. Roll with it."

Samantha couldn't think of anything else to try. "How do we connect with their soul from so far away?"

Whenever Samantha had thought about connecting to

someone's soul, she thought of her husband and late-night conversations that ended up in the bedroom. Or with her sister, after sharing a childhood together and still being joined at the hip into adulthood. Or with her son, who lived inside her long before he was introduced to the world.

But standing on the edge of a mystical river and somehow connecting with a woman she hadn't seen in twenty years who she was actively mad at? That seemed like an impossible task.

"We'll have to connect with the few memories we have with her," Kathy explained. "She's our mother. We have a connection, whether you like it or not right now. You, specifically, have a lot of memories with her. A lot more than I do, at least. You *have* to do this. You have a stronger connection to her than me."

Samantha could see the sadness in her sister's eyes and she felt a little guilty for having memories with their mother before her death—the first time. No matter how Samantha currently felt about her mother, she couldn't let her sister down. Not if it meant throwing something away that Kathy longed for deep within her own soul.

"No," Samantha said. "I can't do it."

Kathy's shoulders slumped. "Then she'll be stuck. Forever. Literally."

Samantha took her hand. "I meant, I can't do it alone. Together, we can."

The younger sister smiled. "But I don't have as many memories as you."

"I don't care. You have some. And even if you don't remember her from before, like you said, we're her daughters. The connection is already there."

They shared another smile, then turned and faced the river. Each of them closed their eyes, recalling memories from so long ago. Holidays and birthdays and dinners and vacations. Reading stories and movie nights and falling asleep on their mother's shoulder. The safety they felt, the *trust* they felt.

Samantha felt her heart warm to her mother. Deep inside, there were happy memories. There was love. And despite recent events, there would always be love.

As the memories flooded their minds, Samantha felt a warmth on her face, growing in intensity as her thoughts ran deeper. Slowly, she opened her eyes as she felt a warm orb settle into her outstretched palm, emitting supernaturally bright light. Once it landed in her hand, the light subsided, leaving a brilliantly-bright white ball in her hand.

Their mother's soul.

CHAPTER 37

The house was quiet for once. Steven was out with Ryan. The two cousins were finally enjoying some time together, after spending the previous few days having all of their plans spoiled. And Kathy was getting Josh up from his nap upstairs.

Meanwhile, Samantha sat in the living room and studied the white orb that she had set on the table. There was a spell in the book to allow spirits to move on. Typically, it was meant for ghosts or other spirits, but the sisters figured it would work for their mother as well. But Samantha couldn't bring herself to allow her mother's soul to move on. Not just yet. They still had unfinished business between them.

But none of that was going to be resolved if Samantha sat

here for even a moment longer. Perched casually on the couch, Samantha recited aloud the spell that had been floating through her mind for the last twenty minutes.

Departed spirit before me,
I release you now and set you free.

Even with the sun streaming through the windows, the room illuminated brighter than ever. Just as quickly as the light came, it passed and Marie stood before her daughter.

Marie offered a sad smile. "Samantha."

She nodded to the chair on the other side of the coffee table. "Sit. We need to talk."

As the departed witch sat, she said, "I hope you know how sorry I am for what I did."

"You realize I can't ever forgive you for that. You put my son in jeopardy"

Marie wiped at a tear on her face. "I know. And I don't expect you to forgive me. You're an excellent mother, Samantha. And good mothers will go to war for their children."

She couldn't argue with that. "And I will in a heartbeat if anyone ever endangers him again. But even if I can't forgive you for that, I think it's time that I forgave you for leaving us twenty years ago."

They studied each other. The surprise was evident on

Marie's face.

Samantha cleared her throat. "That's something that has been bothering me ever since you came back. I tried to pretend like it was great that you returned to us, but deep down I knew it wasn't right. Worse, I still blamed you for all of the hardship Kathy and I went through after you left. After Dad left."

"Your father never told you that I was manipulated into…" Her words trailed off. Even in her second death, she couldn't utter the words *kill myself*. Twenty years later, and the regret was evident.

"He didn't talk much about it. He talked more about your life—when I asked." Samantha shook her head. "I never had the heart to ask. I was too busy being mad at you. Kathy, on the other hand, talked to him a lot about you. Apparently."

As if on cue, the stairs squeaked as Kathy came down with Josh in her arms. At the sight of Marie, she shifted her body so that Josh was as far away from his grandmother as possible.

"Is this the final goodbye?"

Samantha looked down at the floor. She wasn't sure how she felt, now that she had the chance to offer her mother a proper goodbye. "It is."

Marie looked between the three of them. Tears sprung from her eyes, but she smiled as she watched them. "I'm going to miss you all."

Kathy sniffled. "I'm going to miss you too. I loved getting to know you."

"And I loved seeing the women you two have become. I'm so very proud of you both."

Samantha remained silent. She could feel both her mother's and her sister's eyes on her. When she finally looked up, she saw that even Josh was looking at her.

"I just hope that, in time, you'll be able to let me back into your heart, Samantha," Marie said. "I really do love you. Don't you ever doubt that."

Samantha nodded.

"I have a question before you go," Kathy said.

Marie smiled. "Anything, dear. What is it?"

"What happened to Dad? Where is he?"

Her smile faltered. "Well…he's safe. He's well. And he never intended to abandon you."

Samantha scoffed. "Yeah, but he still did."

"No. *I'm* the one who abandoned you both," Marie corrected. "Your father stayed. He was your father. Your only parent. He raised you. The two of you are who you are because of him. If you're going to hold anger for your parents, then hold it against me. When I took my own life, I made all of yours harder. And even when I had the chance to make amends, I made things worse by doing the unspeakable to my only grandchild." She shook her head. "Your father would never do anything like that."

"Mom…" Kathy started, but Samantha shot daggers at her with her eyes.

Necromancer

Marie offered a sad smile. "Our family may not have the story that your father and I envisioned for you girls, but there's no doubt that we both love you dearly. Never forget that."

PICK UP **INCUBUS**, THE NEXT BOOK IN THE **COVEN** SERIES AND LET THE FIGHT CONTINUE!
DAVIDNETHBOOKS.COM/COVEN

ACKNOWLEDGMENTS

This project would not have been possible without the support of my Kickstarter backers! Thank you all for your support!

Sarah B.

Gee Rothvoss

Leslie Twitchell

Marlene Renteria

Samantha Newberry

Dead Fish Books

Rowan Stone

Lou Paduano

John Idlor

Gary Phillips

Shanon M. Brown

Thank you to the DN Publishing VIP Club members over at Patreon!

Tracy O'Neil

Marguerite Goosby

patreon.com/DNPublishing

Eat your heart out.

When Kathy meets Charlie at the library, the two have instant chemistry. The only problem is that he's quite a bit older than her. Despite that, Kathy finds herself falling for Charlie. Hard.

Meanwhile, Samantha is wrapped up in her own marital woes that distract her from noticing just how much Kathy is giving up for her new boyfriend. When she finally does notice, she discovers that Charlie is actually an incubus who intends to impregnate Kathy and take her back to his coven to bear his children.

The only problem is that Kathy is already under his spell.

Incubus is the twelfth book in the Coven series, which is part of the Art of Magic universe, containing the Lost By Magic and the Under the Moon series.

INCUBUS

COVEN: BOOK 12

Read on for an excerpt of the next book in
the Coven series!

DAVID NETH

CHAPTER 1

- July 1990 -

Orias lay back on his bed, lined with red satin sheets while one of his succubi fed him grapes. Another succubus was at his feet, massaging them with her hands. A third stood by and cooed at him, pointing her pouty lips in his direction and giggling whenever he smiled at her.

Rusalka entered his chambers with a stricken look on her face.

"Hello, my darling," Orias said in greeting. "It's so nice to see you. What seems to be upsetting you?"

She held back tears. Out of all the succubi in Orias's harem, Rusalka was the youngest.

"I have failed you," she said.

Orias waved away the other succubi who had been fawning

over him and sat up. "What do you mean, my dear?"

"You have sent me to find a man who would help me make a child. I did as you asked. I found a mate, I seduced him to have sex with me, but I'm afraid there isn't a child inside me. I know that for certain."

Orias stood and approached Rusalka. He placed a hand on her stomach and closed his eyes, sensing for life in her womb.

When he opened his eyes, he announced, "It's true. She is barren."

There were collective gasps from around the room. Each of the succubi stared at each other with worry and curiosity. Each of the demons in the harem had given birth to a child—or several—within their lifetimes. Many of the children had been traded for protection, or taken for the seductive powers they would eventually possess—whether they were incubi or succubi.

"Listen to me," Orias said to his ladies. "Our coven is growing older. Rusalka was the last succubus to produce another child to ensure the longevity of our coven. Without her child, we are facing an uncertain future."

The worried murmurs throughout the room increased. Without children to trade for protection—or to take care of them as they aged further—the coven would surely die off if all of the succubi could no longer produce children.

"Unless," Orias spoke up again, "we do something about this."

"But what are we going to do?" Rusalka asked. "I was the last hope."

"While it's true that the fertility in all of you has reached the end of its limit, my own fertility has no end," he announced. "As the only incubus in our coven, it is my duty to protect you all. And, if by providing that protection, that means leaving you all momentarily so that *I* can find a mate to provide us a child, then so be it."

More gasps filled the room, followed by protests. None of the succubi liked the idea of their incubus being with anyone other than someone from their coven.

"I know this is not the ideal solution, but it is our only choice to secure the future of our line," Orias said. "We will survive!"

CHAPTER 2

- WEDNESDAY -

Samantha rolled her eyes as her husband grumbled on the other end of the couch. She knew his thoughts on coming to see Dr. Bradford, but she didn't care. Their marriage was in trouble and so far, all of their attempts to reconcile weren't working.

"Good morning," Dr. Bradford said in greeting. "It's nice to meet both of you. I'm glad you decided to come and see me today."

Steven scoffed. "I bet."

She swatted at him. "Would you cut it out?"

He shrugged. "Sorry, but I just don't see why I needed to take the day off for this."

"Are you saying that you don't think your marriage is

important enough to take time off of work?" Dr. Bradford asked.

"Not, that's not what I'm saying," Steven said. "I just think that what's going on between a man and his wife should *stay* between a man and his wife."

"Except, we've tried that approach and it's still not working," Samantha countered. "Can you honestly sit there and tell me you've been happy lately?"

He crossed his arms and looked around at the books lining Dr. Bradford's office.

"Exactly!"

Dr. Bradford took a deep breath in order to quiet the bickering couple. "Why don't we start by identifying what the two of you view to be the problem in your marriage?"

"There isn't a problem—"

"He's been so distant and—"

"She's been so wrapped up in thinking that—"

"We *don't* talk, we just argue—"

Dr. Bradford held up his hand to stop them. "Why don't we try one at a time?" He pointed to Steven. "Why don't you start?"

"Honestly? I don't think we even need to be here. Samantha's the one who is so hyper-focused on destroying our marriage since our son was born. We were doing fine until all-of-a-sudden, I'm not doing *this* right and why'd I have to do it *that* way and I should just *know* what she expects from me. It's like, all of a sudden, she's determined to find fault with me."

Samantha's eyes grew wide. "I resent that! Yes, I may be more critical since Josh has been born, but that's only because I realize that we have an impressionable child watching us and seeing the examples we set for what a good person is and what a good marriage is. Honestly, I think we can both do better, but apparently *I'm* the only one who cares."

"Samantha, let's try to refrain from accusations," Dr. Bradford put in. "However, I do think it's a fair point to adjust your *attitudes* when you bring a child into the world. Naturally, as humans, our perceptions change. The child's needs come first a lot of the time, but that doesn't mean we can neglect other needs as well, such as the needs of our spouse. Now, before we move on, Samantha, is there anything else you'd like to share about what *you* think the trouble with your marriage is—again, let's try to keep the accusations to a minimum."

She let out a deep breath and crossed her arms as well. "I just get frustrated when I seem to be the only one—a lot of the times—who is working on our marriage. I'm the one who is worried about how I'm treating Steven or what I say to him and trying to find ways for us to spend time together away from Josh, but also find ways for us to spend time together as a family of three. And all of this on top of running the household and going to work."

Dr. Bradford nodded and turned to Steven. "Do you wish to offer a rebuttal? You said you think your marriage is doing okay. What do you think about Samantha's concerns?"

Steven shrugged. "I guess things *did* used to be easier between us, but we also just had a baby. There's an adjustment period. We'll figure it out."

The room fell into silence as Dr. Bradford studied the two of them. "When was the last time the two of you had sex?"

Samantha and Steven both stared at him in disbelief. Samantha felt a bit exposed for the shift in conversation to be such an intimate part of their lives.

"Has it been so long that neither of you can recall the last time?" he asked. "I know it's an uncomfortable question, but also a very important one."

"Well…" Steven started, then turned to Samantha to finish.

She nodded slowly. "We've…done it several times since Josh was born."

"And did you both enjoy it?"

Samantha crossed her legs and turned to look at her husband to take this next uncomfortable question.

Steven didn't say anything.

"I think the two of you need to readjust your thinking on your marriage," Dr. Bradford suggested. "Typically, when we're young and start dating, we're still living with family and so our partners are our escape from the world. Romantic dates are times for us to relax and unwind. We often don't notice that when we get married, things begin to shift. We initially think, 'Ah, this is great! I get to spend all of my time with this person.' And then the children come." He smiled widely. "And that's when we return to the idea of family and escapism. Not only is your partner someone you're sharing a family with, but they need to continue to be your escape from the responsibilities of the world. *Date* each other again, as if you were teenagers. And never stop."

"So…that's it?" Steven asked. "Your suggestion, at $100 an hour, is to go on a date?"

Samantha smacked his leg and furrowed her brow at him.

Dr. Bradford smiled. "Yes, for now. You need to reconnect with one another. *Talk* to each other. Enjoy each other's company. Connect intimately again so that you refuel the drive and the passion between you. That will make being partners in life so much more easier."

"So you're saying, just like, go to dinner or something?" Samantha asked.

"Go to dinner, go for a long walk, see a movie, whatever it is that the two of you enjoy doing together, do it," the doctor explained. "Find joy in each other's company again. Do you think that's manageable?"

Both Steven and Samantha nodded.

"Good," Dr. Bradford said with a smile. "Then that's your homework. Go on a date—or several—and try to reconnect…*intimately*. If you can do that, and prioritize each other again, you'll rediscover the importance of communicating with one another. It won't happen immediately, but little-by-little, you'll start to see improvements in your lives. Understood?"

Again, both of them nodded.

"Good. I'll see you again on Monday."

CHAPTER 3

- WEDNESDAY -

The library was one of Kathy's favorite places, ever. She loved walking between the stacks of books, being surrounded by the possibilities of a million different stories, words, turns of phrases. Not only that, but the historic library brought her comfort with it's tall ceilings, intricate moulding details, and dark wooden panels. She loved the idea of so many people co-existing in a space, and yet having it be quiet enough to be able to focus and reflect on a million different thoughts.

At the moment, Kathy was perusing books on editing and writing. It was a skillset that she wanted to be able to expand on, considering that she didn't have very many marketable skills for employers.

She reached up to put a book back on the shelf, but as she did the book pushed back another book that slid too far back on the shelf before she could catch it. It pushed into the books on the opposite side of the metal shelf and knocked those books back onto the floor in the next aisle.

"Whoa!" a man shouted on the other side.

Kathy rushed around the stack and saw several books scattered on the floor around a man who was rubbing his head. "I'm *so* sorry! I was putting a book back and it pushed the other ones back—are you okay?" She knelt down and began to pick up the books that had fallen.

"No harm done." He knelt down next to her to help. "Although, I have to admit that I never expected to be attacked in the library."

She rose to her feet, balancing books in her hands, and laughed at his joke.

The two of them locked eyes and Kathy forced herself to look away.

"So…architecture, huh?" She turned and started resolving the books. Idly, she wondered if it would be better to just take them to the checkout desk and explain what had happened so a librarian could make sure they were put away properly.

"Yes, it's an interest of mine." He handed her the books as she shelved them.

"Are you an architect?" She made sure the books were all

neatly arranged on the shelf and in order according to the Dewey Decimal System.

"Unfortunately, no," he said. "But I've always been a fan of design. I have to admit that I'm not very artistic, myself. I'm much more of a numbers person, but art has always intrigued me. Perhaps it's because it's out of my skillset."

"I can understand that. You have an appreciation for it because you know how difficult it is."

"That's a nice way of putting it." He smiled at her.

Now that the books were put away, she had nothing to distract herself with. She searched for a polite way to exit, but couldn't come up with one.

"Are you an artist?" he asked. "Or creative in any way."

Kathy choked out a nervous laugh. "An artist? *No.* But I love reading…and I've always wanted to write a book." She shrugged. "I just haven't committed myself to sitting down and writing one yet."

"You should." He chuckled. "Trust me, at my age, you understand how short life really is and how quickly you'll grow to regret things."

"How old *are* you?" The question fell out of her mouth before she could stop herself. As soon as she heard it, her eyes grew wide and she clamped a hand over her mouth. "I'm sorry! I shouldn't have asked that!"

He laughed. "No, it's okay. I'm not offended. I'm fifty-two."

"*Fifty-two*?" Again, the words left her mouth without consulting with her brain first. "Sorry. I'm just surprised. You don't look that old."

Suddenly shy, he smiled and looked at the books on the shelf. "Well, thank you for that."

As she studied him, though, she finally saw the salt-and-pepper in his beard and the sides of his head, she saw the wrinkles near his eyes and around his mouth, and when he looked in her eyes again, she saw the wisdom that came with age.

"I'm twenty-three." It was her way of cutting off whatever interest was bubbling between them. They had both been flirting, that was for sure, but an almost thirty-year age gap was too much. They had no future together.

And yet, Kathy still felt the attraction between them.

He extended his hand. "I'm Charles Parrish, but I'd like you to call me Charlie."

She took his hand. "Nice to meet you, Charlie. I'm Kathy."

After they shook, he maintained his grip on her hand. "I need to get going, but I just wanted to thank you for not officially killing me today."

Her eyes fluttered to the books, then back to him as she smiled. "Yeah, sorry again about that."

"Maybe we can not kill each other again sometime." He pulled his hand back.

"Maybe."

Incubus

"It was nice meeting you, Kathy." He began to walk backward, down the aisle. "Take care."

She waved and watched him walk away.

To read the rest of **Incubus**,
order your copy at
DavidNethBooks.com/Coven

FIND ALL THE BOOKS IN THE COVEN SERIES!

More by the Author

To find more books by the author, visit
DavidNethBooks.com/Books

* * *

Subscribe to his newsletter to be the first to know of new
releases and special deals!
DavidNethBooks.com/Newsletter

* * *

**If you enjoyed the book, please consider leaving a
review on Goodreads or the retailer you bought it from.**
Reviews help potential readers determine whether
they'll enjoy a book, so any comments on what you
thought of the story would be very helpful!

ABOUT THE AUTHOR

David Neth is the author of the Coven series, the Under the Moon series, Heat series, the Fuse series, and other stories. He lives in Batavia, NY, where he dreams of a successful publishing career and opening his own bookstore.

Also writes small town romance as D. Allen.

www.DavidNethBooks.com

www.facebook.com/DavidNethBooks

www.ingramcontent.com/pod-product-compliance
Lightning Source LLC
Chambersburg PA
CBHW061348310726
48974CB00001B/252